I0518325

Through a Keyhole, Darkly

Darkly

Tales from the Angels' Share

Volume 1

Marella Sands

Word Posse

Dedication
For fellow whiskey fan Keith;
There's probably a 12-year Glenlivet around here we can share.

Acknowledgements
Thanks to everyone who helped put this manuscript together:
Brian Pigg, Sue Bradford Edwards, Sharon Shinn, Rett MacPherson,
Deborah Millitello, Mark Sumner, Tom Drennan, and Laurell K. Hamilton.

From Word Posse
Sleeping the Churchyard Sleep, Rett MacPherson
Pandora's Mirror, Marella Sands
Fortune's Daughter, Marella Sands
Restless Bones, Marella Sands
Through a Keyhole, Darkly: Tales from the Angels' Share, Volume 1,
Marella Sands
The Water Girl, Deborah Millitello
Do Virgins Taste Better? And Other Strange Tales, Deborah Millitello
Thor McGraw and the Ice Man Murder, Tom Drennan
The Naturalist, Mark Sumner
On Whetsday, Mark Sumner

Visit us at www.wordposse.com

This book has been typeset in Fanwood. Cover design by Word Posse. Photos by Golden Mean Photography.

ISBN-13:978-1-944089-11-5

Praise for *Restless Bones*

"Marella Sands has a keen eye for detail, and an ability to take innocent research and bits of trivia, and turn them into stories that will disturb, frighten, charm, and make you think." Laurell K. Hamilton

"Intense! An exciting variety of stories. I had to remind myself to breathe." Cari Mahoney

"The quality of the writing here is superb. I really loved the book, and I can easily say these are some of the best horror stories I have ever read. I will definitely read this book again." Laura L. Davison

"Restless Bones is a must read for lovers of literary horror fiction and classic tales of dark drama and fantasy. This book falls into that rare group that tells unexpected and original stories that don't rely on clichés or overused plot devices. The short story length keeps you interested from beginning to end, and if you are like me, you'll find you just want to keep reading all the way through to the last one." Layla Messing

"I think Marella Sands may have made a horror short-story fan out of me! The writing was top-quality—a good amount of details and lyrical prose that added to the scenery without bogging it down." Kaylee Stevens

"Haunting and engrossing, this compilation of tales of spine-tingling horror will have you on the edge of your seat, hiding beneath the covers, and leave you wanting more. I was surprised to finish it so quickly, but I didn't want to stop reading once I started!" Brenda Maxwell

"The way Sands uses language to create emotion and describe scenery is impressive, and the characters are believable and well-developed. The stories are a great length to read in one sitting—if you can take it! I had goose bumps throughout. Can't wait to read more from Marella Sands." Nicole Hastings

"I really enjoyed this book as a whole, and thought each story was as good as (if not better than) the one before. It's hard to pick a favorite. Great writing and characterizations. A must read for fans of horror and dark fantasy." Stacy Decker

"I generally reserve my more effusive praise for long, epic novels that I feel have completely consumed me and hijacked my brain and soul for a time. But today I will be making an exception. [Restless Bones is] dark, disturbing, and not for the faint of heart. I was surprised by the amount of emotion and investment the author manages to pull from the reader in just a few pages. Will definitely be checking out works from Sands in the future, and will recommend to my friends." Darlene Cupp

"As a huge reader of books, and most of them indie or small-press published, I've pretty much accepted the fact that there will be certain things that won't be up to the same standards as the big press published books. However, I was pleasantly surprised by the top-notch professionalism in this book, from the flawless editing to the strength of the narration and the complexity of the characters and engaging storylines—a real challenge considering the shorter length of these stories. This horror anthology is one of the better ones I've read. Kudos to Ms. Sands for raising the bar; she will be on my list of authors to watch." Max Gilbert

Praise for *Fortune's Daughter*

"A delightful story, full of mystery, magic, romance, and a bit of steampunk. Perfect for young adult readers and lovers of cross-genres. I can't wait to read more stories about this world and the people in it." Beth Bancroft

"A beautifully written tale of a woman whose choices will lead her society into a new age. The need to find out what happens will keep you up well past your bedtime." Heather Clark-Evans

"I've got my fingers crossed that this might become a series. Please, please tell me this is Book One!" Cheryl Medley

Praise for *Pandora's Mirror*

"I am most certainly glad I took the chance on Pandora's Mirror. *This was a brilliant novel and very well-crafted. I liked that the characters were paranormal investigators, as I've never read a book with those before. But I was most impressed with the amazing writing—literary, beautiful, almost poetic prose that made the story even creepier to read! Intelligent and intricate with parts that made me literally gasp out loud."* Essie Harmon

"This has the elements of a horror story, but it is also has a romance, a tragedy, a mystery, and the paranormal. The writing is stellar. I was really impressed with the great editing too (I notice things like that). Fans of the show Ghost Hunters *will eat it up, as will anyone who enjoys a scary, well-written mystery with a ghostly vibe."* Max Gilbert

"The writing is simply lovely, with literary prose that has powerful, evocative word choices that truly bring this terrifying story to life. A fast read with shocking twists, and a satisfying ending." Nicole Hastings

"Warning—when starting Pandora's Mirror, *make sure you don't have anywhere you need to be or anything you need to do because you won't want to stop reading until you've finished it all!"* Stacy Decker

1

The key showed up at midnight.

I'd been talking with Fish, one of the regulars at the Angels' Share bar. He was a fixture here, as alcohol-filled and shabby around the edges as the place itself. Fish liked to tell stories of all the fabulous adventures he'd had as a boy; apparently, in one lifetime, he'd managed to be a pirate, a gigolo, a doorman, a graphic artist, a battlefield surgeon, and even a sponge diver. I went along with it, like everyone else. Fish told good stories, and even if he sometimes mixed them up, no one cared.

I liked Fish. He never hit on me the way some guys do when they see a female bartender, and he never said stupid shit like "Hey, Teryl, what's a pretty girl like you doing in a place like this?" In fact, he'd never asked me about my past, which I was grateful for. Fish took me exactly as I presented myself, and didn't worry about what darkness or pain might be lurking underneath. He always had more stories to tell about himself, anyway.

So it was odd that, when I turned back to the bar and saw the key shining dully on the bartop, almost glowing under the dim yellow light of the unreliable overhead fixtures, and looked to Fish to see if it belonged to him, he shrugged. Fish is not known for being quiet when there's a story to be told.

"Not yours?" I asked as I picked it up. It was a small brass key, perhaps something that might go to a post office box or a private locker.

"Would it be sitting there waiting for you to toss it in the trash if it were?" Fish actually sounded a bit disgusted, and I couldn't imagine how a key could prompt such a reaction. None of my business, though.

I threw the thing away. It landed on the heap of cocktail napkins, maraschino cherries, and beer bottles that filled the trash bin under the bar.

Fish pushed his glass forward and I raised my eyebrow, unsure what he wanted besides more alcohol. Most people stick to their favorite, but Fish got his nickname for a reason: he not only drank like a fish, he drank everything in his environment. And in a bar, that meant *everything*. Tonight, he'd had a mojito, a Long Island iced tea, a shot of tequila, a PBR, and two whiskey sours. Don't ask me how he stayed upright. I assumed he had a liver of steel.

"Jack," he said. "A double." I obligingly gave him the requested liquor and he sipped it as if it were ambrosia.

I put away the Jack and noticed one of the guys in the corner booth waving at me. The two of them had been drinking Jameson's all evening, and, like Fish, they seemed determined to leave with exhausted livers.

I walked over. "Can I get you gentlemen anything else?" The larger of the two stared at his empty glass, but the other, the one who had waved, shook his head. "We're ready to pay up."

"All right."

I figured out their tab and took it to their table. The smaller man looked at the total, sighed, and brought out a wallet. "Nothing gets cheaper over time, does it?" he said. The question seemed rhetorical; his companion didn't answer, and he wasn't looking at me, so I waited for him to hand me the money.

He counted out the bills with quick, bird-like movements and laid twenty dollars too much in front of me. "Keep it," he said before I could ask.

He put the wallet away and ran a hand through his short black hair. His companion finally looked up; his eyes were bloodshot. It would seem at least one of them was feeling the effects of an evening spent throwing down whiskey.

Strange that it was the guy with more bulk who was the most toasted, but some people had more tolerance than others. You could never tell who would pass out after a single drink, and who could suck down a bottle and walk out steady as a rock.

The two of them got up and headed for the door. Now that I could see the other side of the larger man's face, I noticed his ear was a ragged mess. It looked like an old injury; maybe he'd been in the military, or in a bad fight.

Well, there was a story behind every customer of a bar like this. It was not the kind of place people without troubles chose to hang out.

I pocketed the money and went back to the bar. Now that the two men were gone, it was me and Fish and an hour until closing time.

Fish, I knew, wouldn't leave until the bossman shoved him out the door.

I got my damp rag and went to the corner booth to wipe down the table and remove the trash the two men had left behind. The table didn't take more than a few moments of my time. The two men had been much neater than most clients.

I went back to the bar and put the men's glasses in the sink. I glanced over at Fish to see if he'd finished his drink and if he'd request another. But he was merely staring sadly at the art hanging to the right of the bar, next to the boss' office door. Fish had told me once who the artist was, but I couldn't remember a name so long and Italian. The painting seemed to depict angels falling out of an attic onto people's heads or something. When I'd said that out loud, though, Fish had laughed at me. That had been the one time I'd truly gotten angry with him. He didn't have to mock me for not knowing about old art.

All the art in the bar was angel-related. I'd assumed that was to go with the bar's name: *Angels' Share*. That was what distillers called the whiskey that evaporated out of the barrels during the years it was aging. The liquid which had soaked into the wood of the barrel itself was the *devil's cut*. The remainder—whatever the angels and the devil didn't get—was what got bottled.

Fish sighed and looked away from the painting. He was lanky, with fingers so long you figure his parents must have shelled out for piano lessons at some point. He was angular and pale, with short brown hair tinged with red which he moussed straight up, as if it were shocked about something and were trying to escape his scalp. His clothes were sloppy and overlarge, and made him look even thinner than he was. His shoes were threads away from losing all structural integrity.

Despite looking like a hobo, Fish always had money to drink away. Sometimes I wondered where he got the money, but I didn't ask. I didn't really want to know.

Fish generally had an ageless quality, with unlined skin, a complete lack of gray in his hair, and a clear voice. I'd have said he was no more than thirty, except his eyes were often sunken and his demeanor was one of a man weighed down with far more years than Fish could possibly be burdened with. Still. No one who drank like he did could possibly be forty without a crow's foot to be seen.

I went back to the booth to deposit clean coasters decorated with the bar's name in great swooping letters. Now the booth was ready for more customers.

I glanced up as my boss, Ware, poked his head out of his private office briefly. Fish raised a glass to him. Ware nodded in return and disappeared once more into the back room.

As I turned away from the booth, a newspaper in the seat caught my eye. I picked it up. The paper had been folded to show an article on a recent murder. *U City man shot in South City.* I'd heard of that briefly; some customers had mentioned it the other day, but I hadn't paid much attention. Life was hard enough without making it worse by paying attention to the bad things that happened to other people.

I brought the paper back to the bar. Fish glanced over at it, then held out his shot glass to me. With anybody else, I'd be telling them I was cutting them off, but Fish looked as sober as ever. Not for the first time, I wondered if he even *could* get drunk.

"What you got there?" he asked as I took the glass and put it in the sink.

"More trash, unless someone else wants to read it."

Fish scanned the article that had been highlighted and bit his lip. "Sad."

"It's always sad when someone gets shot."

"And dies," he said. "It's always sad when someone dies."

"Oh," I said for lack of anything more coherent. I hadn't read past the headline and I hadn't bothered to learn the details when the incident had been mentioned by customers. I walked around behind the bar and dropped my rag back in its place.

"People don't realize how often the choices they make are reversible," Fish continued. "And then, one day, you're gone. No more chances."

Maybe the guy *could* get drunk and I was finally seeing the Fish that only appeared when the man was pickled. Seemed like he was going to be a morose drunk.

Which was better than angry or violent or disgusting. Morose I could deal with.

I spotted a table with the remains of a martini I hadn't bused yet. I reached for my rag.

It wasn't there.

I looked accusingly at Fish. He must have swiped it somehow without me seeing him do it. Normally, he wasn't the kind who played pranks, but he was so lit he probably had no idea what he was doing. I realized I'd be cutting him off.

There's a first time for everything.

"Come on," I said. "Where's my rag?"

Fish looked up from the paper, which he was still studying. "What rag?" God, he was a talented liar. His manner appeared totally innocent.

"You know what I mean," I said. "It's not funny."

Fish shrugged. "Not me. George." He drained the rest of his Jack.

I took the glass as soon as he placed it on the bar.

He frowned. "Hey, I was considering another one."

"No way. You're toasted. And you're the only other person here, so don't go blaming imaginary people for what you did."

Fish shook his head and frowned. "George may be imaginary, but he's not, really."

"Seriously, what?" I asked in astonishment. "He's imaginary, but he's not imaginary?" For someone who ought to be in an ER suffering from alcohol poisoning, it wasn't so surprising that Fish was experiencing at least *some* effects from all the booze. The unnerving thing was that the lying was the *only* symptom I could discern. His eyes were clear, his hands steady, his words unslurred. The man appeared totally sober.

"Pay up and leave," I said. "You're finished for the evening."

Fish hesitated, then shrugged and reached into his pocket. He pulled out a few bills and placed them on the bar. "It's okay, I get it," he said. "But George will prove me an honest man someday. Hope you get your rag back."

Fish walked out the door as rock-solid as a teetotaler. I swear I had no idea how he did that.

My boss came out of the back as the door slammed behind Fish. "He's leaving before closing time?"

"I cut him off," I said. "He's playing with me and wants to blame it on George."

"Oh." Ware sat down in the creaky stool vacated by Fish. The scent of his aftershave wafted across the bar. Somehow, no matter how late it got, Ware managed to smell as if he'd been indulging in personal grooming. Heck, maybe he spent most of his time in the office preening. People had odd obsessions.

"George gets blamed for a lot."

I shrugged. "I guess." George was the excuse everyone at Angels' Share traditionally used when things went wrong. Did it rain the one day you left your car window rolled down? George did it. Miss your bus? George's fault. Misplace your wallet? George took it.

Normally, I thought this amusing, but not at the moment.

"What did George do now?"

"Took my rag."

Ware shrugged. "We've got more. It's not important."

Yes, we had more rags. That wasn't the point. It bothered me that Fish would take it and lie to me.

Ware glanced at the paper Fish had left behind. "He brought in a paper? I've never pegged him for a reader."

"It's not his. I found it in a booth. Fish read the article on someone being shot, seemed upset that they had died. Started going on about there being no more second chances after death. That's when I cut him off."

"Huh." Ware pushed the paper aside. "No second chances after death. Guess that's true."

Ware was a little shorter than Fish, and far broader. He carried a lot of weight, but did it while remaining light on his feet. Built like a wrestler, moved like a dancer. Since I was a born stumblebum, his innate grace annoyed me.

I had no idea of his age, and the relative lack of wrinkles mixed with the white hair gave conflicting estimates. The most intriguing thing about him was his eyebrows, which were white but tipped in black. I couldn't decide if that made him appear older or younger.

But age wasn't important. What was important was that he was a good boss. He didn't mess with the staff and didn't allow anyone else to, either. One night, when a drunk college kid tried to feel me up while I was busing a table, Ware burst out of his office, hefted the kid by his collar, and threw him into the street.

He paid well, too. He said it was because he couldn't always find good help, so if you found someone you could rely on, you had to pay them decently. I didn't mind making more money than I'd ever done before, but it did seem odd that we needed to replace staff as often as we did. Most of them had worked in bars before, so they were used to the groping, the insults, the puke in the bathroom stalls, and all the other lovely things that went with imbibing excessive quantities of liquor. A boss who'd toss out someone who groped you, and who paid you well, wasn't one to lose lightly.

Not that he was a really friendly guy, but I don't need to be friends with the boss. Let me do my job without hovering and don't abuse me, and we're good. Ware was that in spades.

The only thing that made me nervous was that I'd never been in his office. Not even when he interviewed me for the job. He'd interviewed me in a booth. And when he'd hired me, he'd made it clear that none of the staff was to go past the door marked PRIVATE.

I had never done so, and had no desire to do so. But it did make me wonder what he did back there, and who the people were who occasionally came in and went directly into that room without buying a drink or even glancing around the interior of the bar. They seemed to know exactly where they were going, and what they were in the building for, and nothing could distract them from whatever duty they had there.

The weirdest thing was that I'd never seen anyone come *out* of the office, except Ware. I assumed there was a back entrance, though that didn't explain why people came in the front only to leave by the back.

"You available next Sunday?" Ware asked. "Time and a half pay."

I normally didn't work Sundays, and on Mondays, Ware closed the place up. I wasn't thrilled to work six days in a row, but the money would be useful. "Sure," I said.

"Good. Boyle's got some event to go to. Family reunion, something." Ware shrugged and glanced around the empty bar. "Why don't you head on home for now?"

Closing time wasn't for forty-five minutes, and I still had a martini glass to get bused. Ware saw the direction of my gaze. "Leave it," he said. "I got the Gang coming in tonight, anyway, so cleaning up beforehand is pointless."

The Gang was how Ware described his own drinking buddies. They would come in at closing time every other week or so, sit together in a cluster, and wait for everyone to leave. I hadn't gotten to know them well; they were an insular group. Three men, two women, everyone seemingly middle-aged or a little older, and exceptionally well-spoken. The most exotic was a tall woman with midnight-black skin, hair shaved so short she was nearly bald, and who wore bracelets that covered her arms up to her elbows. The others called her "Little Girl." You'd think she'd be insulted but she appeared to find it hilarious. I guess she was their version of Little John, except I suppose that made Ware Robin Hood, and that didn't really fit him.

"All right." I already knew he wouldn't dock me, since he was the one sending me off. Like I said, he was a good boss. I put the money in the till and took out my tips. Ware didn't even bother to double-check my math, which always made me a little nervous. I had never been great at math, and while I was pretty sure I'd figured out everything correctly, I couldn't swear to it. Still, I certainly wouldn't cheat my boss on purpose.

I glanced down and paled. My rag was there where I'd left it, limp and damp and in the proper place. Ware saw me blanch.

"What's up?"

"Rag's back." I grabbed my wallet, stuffed my tips inside, and walked around the bar. I knew that damn thing hadn't been there two minutes ago.

"Don't worry about it," said Ware flatly. "It's only George."

I didn't have an answer to that.

2

The night was humid but relatively cool. Cool for St. Louis in August, anyway. I'd be sweaty by the time I got to my car, but the sweat wouldn't be from the temperature. Humidity is the worst. Sometimes, I wondered what the first European immigrants to the area had thought of the place: hotter and more humid than Europe in the summer, colder in the winter and dry enough to make your skin crack open. It must have seemed like hell.

To my surprise, I had barely started toward my car when I saw Fish leaning against the decrepit brick building next to the slightly less-decrepit one that housed the bar. He had his hands in his pockets, and his head was down, as if he had nothing better to do than stare at his feet. He looked up as I neared him.

"Leaving early?" he asked with some alarm. "Don't tell me Ware fired you for kicking me out. I'll talk to him if he did." Fish seemed genuinely concerned. For some reason, he appeared more pitiful than usual. Maybe that was just the night air and the fact he seemed so wretched, thinking I'd gotten fired.

"No, no, he decided I could go home early. His buddies are starting to show."

"Ah," he said as if that explained everything. "The Gang." He seemed both amused and disappointed. "I didn't think this was their night."

I leaned against the building next to him and watched a stray cat slink into the space in between the two buildings.

"I wasn't expecting them, but it seems they're coming, anyway. Guess you're not welcome? You're around the bar enough, you'd think at some point they might invite you to join them."

"I don't want an invitation. I'm better off alone. They have an old bond. I wouldn't fit in." His tone was wistful, though, as if he wished there were a group of people he shared that kind of bond with.

Fish nodded back toward the Angels' Share. "They're arriving."

I turned to face the dispirited brick exterior of the Angels' Share. Ware had turned off the neon sign that said OPEN, but a burly figure opened the door and strode right in. I think he was the one the others called Yama, but I couldn't be sure. At least two of the Gang were fairly heavyset men and in the glare of the sodium streetlights, it would be difficult to tell them apart at this distance unless you knew them well. Which I did not.

Fish stared at the bar with an odd intensity, his wretchedness even worse than before, almost palpable in its reality. I got the strange feeling he'd been part of that group, or one very like it, a long time ago. For the first time, I wondered about the stories Fish *didn't* tell about himself.

Another figure strode up to the door, a middle-aged woman in a long flowing skirt and fringed tunic. She looked more like a refugee from Woodstock than anything else, with the shapeless clothes and long straight dark hair. I'd only seen her once before and had no idea what her name might be. She wasn't fat, but she looked solid, like a brick wall. As far as I could recall, she'd never spoken to me, or even looked in my direction. That hadn't bothered me; I found

Little Girl's smile intimidating and honestly would have preferred she'd never noticed me. Who knew what this woman was like?

Still, it would be useful to have a name.

"Who's that?" I asked, wondering if I could get information from Fish. Just because he wasn't a member of the Gang didn't mean he didn't know who they were.

"Lucy," he said.

"Lucy?" I blinked in surprise. "You mean the others have named like Yama and Little Girl and Truck and she's just *Lucy?*"

"It's short for something else."

"Short for what?"

He hesitated, then shrugged. "Melusine. I've never heard her use that name, though. Maybe it sounds too French."

"Nothing can sound too French in St. Louis."

"Point taken," he said with a forced lightness. "Look, if you're headed to your car, I'd be happy to walk you there."

"I walk myself to my car all the time."

He smiled. It was a genuine smile, of the sort I'd never seen on him before, and it held just a hint of mischief. It made him look very young, and it suited him. "You only think you do. Ware keeps an eye on you, you know. Well, all of his employees, really."

My heart thumped at the news. Did my boss really watch me when I left the bar? I'd certainly been happy enough when Ware had thrown that college kid out. Was I happy to know he didn't withdraw that protection at the door?

Then it occurred to me that Fish had been loitering outside for a reason. A reason that had brought Ware out of his office when Fish had departed the bar early.

"You're my escort at night," I said accusingly. I took a step back, both appalled and somewhat gratified. I wanted to think I didn't need any protection, but there was always someone bigger and stronger than you out there. Nobody could get by just on their own. Not even Ware.

On the other hand, Fish hardly seemed like the ideal bodyguard. His thin physique was more gaunt than fit, and though he liked to tell stories about his adventures, I'd never believed he'd actually had any. He seemed like a person too invested in sitting still, in letting the world go by without getting involved. He told tales. He didn't live in them.

Fish looked a bit sheepish. "Yeah, well, I guess I am. Ware pays well." He gave me a hangdog look. "Are you okay with knowing that? Ware will be angry with me if you tell him you're not okay with this."

"Why?"

"Because I'm not supposed to be seen. I'm just supposed to keep an eye on you, make sure you get to your car safely."

I laughed. What was the point in being angry about it? "Oh, what the hell. Sure, it's okay. Let's go, then."

We left the bar behind and walked down the street. As we passed under a streetlamp, I glanced over at Fish and noticed an odd line on his skin, creeping up past his collar toward his neck.

"You never struck me as someone who would get a tattoo," I said.

"What?" He looked over at me with a confused expression, and I pointed toward his shoulder. His demeanor went from curious and confused to withdrawn. His face shuttered, all emotion forced out. "Oh," he said without emotion. "Not a tattoo. A scar."

"What from?"

"Nothing important," he mumbled. "It was a long time ago."

For once, it seemed, we had hit on a topic that shut Fish up. I couldn't recall any tale of his that involved being injured on the shoulder. Clearly, this was something he'd rather tuck away and keep private. I decided not to push.

We got to my car, a little Escort I'd named Nixie. She was reliable and solid, and not flashy enough to attract attention when she was parked on a side street until the wee hours.

I hunted around for something to say to break the mood. "Sorry," I said at last. "I shouldn't have asked. And I shouldn't have accused you of taking my cloth. It's still there. I must have missed it somehow."

"You didn't miss it," said Fish. "I'm sure it was gone. Things happen in that building. Odd things. Some people are more sensitive to them than others."

"You're telling me it's haunted."

"Maybe."

I bit back a sarcastic retort. I was trying to apologize, not start an argument or belittle a man's beliefs.

He continued. "What's *haunted* mean, you know? All I'm saying is odd things happen in that building. People say that it's George, but whether George is a ghost, an alien, a fairy, a time traveling pot-bellied pig, or an odd wrinkle in the space-time continuum is anybody's guess. That's all I meant when I said George was imaginary and also not. Things happen, but you don't need ghosts to explain it, not really. Maybe it's quantum mechanics."

"And how would that explain it?"

"Hell if I know."

3

Fish sidled off into the darkness. I drove home and slunk into the apartment I shared with my boyfriend and my pet hedgehog, Petunia. Castro usually tried to wait up for me, but he'd had a cold lately and I didn't want to wake him if he had managed to fall asleep. So I shut the apartment door and locked it behind me as quietly as I could.

Castro and I had met at a convenience store. We'd stumbled into each other and shared a laugh when it turned out we were buying identical items of microwave popcorn and diet Coke. The laugh was followed by a popcorn-and-movie night, which was followed by sex, which was promptly followed by moving in together. A year later, we were still making it work. Neither of us had done anything as permanent as live with someone before, so it had been new territory for us both. Figuring out how to negotiate the temperature on the thermostat, the use of the shower, and how to determine whose wishes should prevail concerning the position of the toilet seat, had certainly enlivened our early days together.

By now, I knew that he preferred to be alone when ill, to recover in darkness and silence. So instead of checking on him first, I went to the apartment's kitchen, which was occupied by a small table topped with Petunia's cage.

Petunia had been an impulse acquisition at a pet adoption event held at a small, independently owned pet supply store. Castro and I had gone to look for a dog toy for a neighbor's new puppy. While he shopped for the perfect puppy present, I wandered through the rest of the store. I didn't consider myself an animal person, but as I passed by a small cage, I saw Petunia and instantly fell in love. I had no idea anyone kept hedgehogs as pets, but her little nose, square feet, and beady black gaze grabbed me at once and didn't let go. One look and I was a goner.

Fortunately, Castro felt the same, and he babied her. Even when I worked long hours, I knew Petunia would have everything a hedgehog could possibly want. And Petunia returned the affection. In a way, it made me jealous, that I had spotted her first, but her heart belonged to Castro.

Tonight, she gave me a good snuffling and then went back to rooting through her litter. The good thing about a nocturnal pet was that she was always up when I got home, guaranteeing I received an adorable hedgehog greeting every night.

I made sure Petunia had enough food and water, even though I knew Castro would already have done that, and I headed for the fridge. Angels' Share didn't have a kitchen so I didn't eat dinner until after I got home.

A small sob came from down the hall.

"Castro?" My heart dropped. If Castro were sick enough to be crying, he was really sick. He should have called me at work and asked me to come home if he were that bad off.

I rushed to the bedroom and opened the door, heart in my throat. But Castro lay sprawled across the queen bed, only one foot tucked under the comforter. He snored lightly, a welcome relief from previous nights when his cold had him making half-snoring half-choking noises all night. He must be feeling better. My heart settled down. He was okay. The noise must have come from outside.

I went back to the kitchen and told Petunia, "Must be imagining things." She twitched her nose in my direction before going back to her hedgehog business.

I checked the fridge but it was empty. Not a surprise, since Castro was the one who kept it stocked and I hadn't thought to go to the store before my shift. Peanut butter and crackers it was. I opened the cabinet and grabbed the jar of peanut butter.

Another sob. I turned slowly. Petunia had frozen in place and was staring at the hall that led to our apartment's tiny bedroom and nearly microscopic bathroom.

Fuck. I doubt there was any way to share a hallucination with a hedgehog. Somebody really was sobbing here. They must be in the bathroom.

Did they break in? Was it one of Castro's friends whom he sometimes let crash on our couch? That was most likely, but still. I didn't like the odd hollow quality of the sound. Or the way Petunia was frozen in what seemed like fear. She'd never been afraid of anyone in the apartment that I could recall.

It was probably Andre. That guy bounced from girlfriend's pad to girlfriend's pad so often I'd long ago given up trying to figure out who he was shacking up with this week. In between, he sometimes ended up on our couch for a night or two, but then he was right back to his regular routine.

I liked Andre. He was a little on the short side, but cute, and he had an endearing quality that made girls fall all over him. But he had a wandering eye that got him into trouble pretty quickly.

I couldn't recall hearing Andre cry before, even during the worst break-up. I wanted to go to the bathroom and see what was wrong, but something held me in place. As if Petunia's fear had been communicated to me via some kind of interspecies telepathy. I knew this had to be one of Castro's friends. It had to be. No one was going to break into an apartment to sob in a stranger's bathroom.

Yet there was something in the quality of the sound, of the dead silence in the rest of the apartment, in the hedgehog's behavior. Something was off, and some instinct in the back of my mind knew it. It was urging me to run away. To run far, and run fast, as if a tiger were right behind me.

But there was no tiger. Of course there wasn't. There was someone crying. I was spooked only because it was dark, and because of the weird thing that had happened at the Angels' Share. Only that.

I forced one foot in front of the other. Once. Twice. One more step to the bathroom. One more step, but it was the longest step of my life.

Something touched me on the shoulder. I jumped and screamed.

"Whoa!" said Castro. "What the fuck?"

I whirled and pushed him against the wall. My heart pounded so hard, I was sure it was going to break out of my ribcage. Or fling itself up my throat. "You scared me!"

"What?" he asked again. His short black hair stood out at all angles and his several-days growth of beard gave him a rakish look. Dark brown eyes were bloodshot and blinked rapidly at the light coming in from the streetlamp outside.

"Someone's in the apartment," I said. "They're in the bathroom." At his dubious expression, I continued, "I heard someone crying in there."

He shook his head. "Nobody's here. And besides," he glanced down at my hands, "you were going to assault them with half a jar of peanut butter? You know they make those out of plastic these days."

"I heard someone," I insisted.

He grunted and took the step I had been unable to. "Yo!" he called out as he flipped on the light.

I waited, breathless, while the yellow light streamed from the bathroom made me blink as badly as Castro.

"No one's in here," he said. "Hey, this yours?" He turned around and held out his hand. In it was a key.

It was the same key I had thrown away at the Angels' Share.

My heart did another somersault. "That's not mine," I whispered. "It's not."

"Oh," said Castro. He held it up to his face and twirled it around idly. "Well, it's not mine."

"Someone was here," I said.

"No one's here."

"Then where did the key come from?"

He shrugged. "I'm on so much over-the-counter cold medication, I could have put it there and forgotten about it. Seriously. No one's here. You coming to bed?"

I looked down at the peanut butter jar. I couldn't imagine eating any of it tonight. At the moment, hunger was as alien as the key in Castro's hand.

"Guess so."

I went back to the kitchen and put the peanut butter away. Petunia was busy rooting through her litter as if nothing had frightened her at all.

I went to bed and tried to relax. Castro dozed off almost immediately, one arm draped over my stomach. But in my mind, I kept hearing the sobbing over and over, and the sound would not let me sleep.

4

Because Castro hadn't restocked while he was sick, breakfast was a skimpy affair of toast and oatmeal. "Bacon and eggs need to go on the list," I said as I crunched my perfectly browned toast. Just because we didn't have the good stuff didn't mean what was left had to be over- or underdone.

"Sure," said Castro. He looked much better than he had in days. An almost-uninterrupted night's sleep had done wonders for him. He added, "And I'll pick up milk, cheese, Pop-Tarts, lunch meat, bread, chocolate. All the usual suspects."

I felt more able to deal with the weird aspects of the night now that the bright morning light was streaming in to our dingy apartment. "Where did that key go that you found last night?"

He waved his mug of coffee toward the front door. "On the table by the couch."

I finished my toast and went to the other room. The table sat right by the door and was usually where we dropped our keys and the mail. The key depository was a crappy clay bowl I'd made in elementary school.

Three pennies sat in the bottom of the bowl. They'd been there for weeks. But the key? I looked around the room. Tired ancient furniture, a threadbare throw rug, and a rickety chair we'd rescued from the Dumpster outside our apartment building constituted the remaining items in the room.

"Nope," I said. "Not there."

"Has to be," said Castro. He sauntered out of the kitchen, still clutching the mug. I showed him the three pennies in the bowl. He shrugged. "Huh. Guess I forgot where I put it. Weird that it was a key, though."

I put the bowl down. "Weird how?"

"Been reading the news lately," he said.

I nodded. Castro wasn't a big reader of fiction, but he was an insatiable consumer of weird news, especially if someone died. And the more bizarre the circumstances, the more he'd read about it. For two days last year, I'd had to hear about a guy who'd been shot, stabbed twice in the back, and then had *no escape* written on his body with a Sharpie. Castro had seemed to be delighted with the copywriter's insistence that "the police were baffled." He'd laughed out loud, and said, "No shit—because crap like that happens *every day!*"

I guess he'd found another interesting death in the papers this week.

"Guy was shot to death, not too far from where you work, actually. He had a key no one recognized. The paper was going to show an image of it for anyone to call in with any information, but it went missing."

"What? Why would that even be important?" Despite the weird twist the news gave my gut, this meant nothing. Everybody carried keys around.

"Well, he had a house key and a car key and a key to his girlfriend's place and a key to his mother's place. And then there was this other key. It was tucked into his wallet, too, not on his keychain. The police think he was having an affair, though the girlfriend says he'd never do that. Other people think he was stashing drug money somewhere. The girlfriend insists he wouldn't have anything to do with drugs, either."

"Okay, but why mention it in the article? Surely people can have random keys on them."

He shrugged. "Guess maybe it's because his other keys were taken, and found in a Dumpster nearby. Then there's this mysterious key in his wallet. Wouldn't you think it would be the other way around—steal the wallet, leave the keys?"

"Maybe they wanted his car and then panicked."

"Mm," he said as he downed the last of his coffee. "Whatever. I'm going to take a shower, then head out to the store."

"All right." I pulled out my phone and realized I hadn't charged it last night. "Guess charging my phone is first order of business. Can I borrow yours?"

"Sure." He put the cup down in the kitchen, blew Petunia a kiss, and headed for the bathroom.

I wandered into the bedroom and scooped up Castro's phone, plopped onto the bed, and started reading the articles he'd located on the murder.

The first article was skimpy on details of the murder of the man, who was identified as Marco Kendall, but did quote the girlfriend, who was identified as Cara Diaz, as saying, "I don't know why he was in that neighborhood. We don't know anyone there."

Another article spent more time on the location of the murder, which was indeed near the Angels' Share. One article mentioned a cut on the victim's right hand, which the police were calling a defensive wound.

I'd only read a few articles before Castro returned. He took showers at light speed. He claimed that was due to years of living in foster homes where he was allowed only a few minutes to get ready for school or bed without incurring the wrath of his foster parents. I would have thought that would have led to him taking extraordinarily long showers once he left the foster system behind, but he said the habit was too hard to break.

He'd shaved, though I had to admit, I was missing the skimpy beard he'd grown over the past week. Perhaps I'd be able to convince him to grow it back.

Castro pulled out his standard outfit of jeans and a t-shirt. I loved to watch him get dressed; his movements were fluid and elegant, but at the same time a little awkward, as if he were embarrassed by his own gracefulness. One of his foster mothers had put him in ballet classes for a couple of years, and I had always thought it was because she had recognized this quality in him. Castro said it was just because she'd like to see him squirm under the dance instructor's strict tutelage. He had few nice things to say about any of his foster parents.

If there were any rebellion in Castro at all, it manifested in his inability to hold down a job for any length of time. Five minute showers were too much a habit to break, but having to be on time for something every day was a habit he'd been more than happy to put down once he was on his own. I couldn't complain too much, though, because he did all our shopping, took care of Petunia, handled the laundry, and cleaned up after himself. Andre thought Castro's homemaking abilities were somehow a detriment to his desirability, but I was happy enough to be the one earning the money if he'd scrub toilets and figure out which detergent was on sale this week and what coupon could get us another twenty cents off chips or toothpaste.

You had to appreciate a guy who, when you came home, smelled of bleach or the cat food he'd been putting into Petunia's bowl. And who didn't blow the money you brought home on cigarettes or liquor. So he didn't bring home a regular paycheck. He had plenty of qualities I admired.

Sometimes I wondered if that were enough to keep us together, but who the hell knew? I'd never tried living with someone before, and neither had he. We were running on instinct and guesswork, and I had no idea how long those two things would keep us afloat. Mostly, I just prayed we would continue to be good to each other. Neither of us had had much of that growing up, and if what we had wasn't the eternally passionate love of romance novels, it was solid and comforting.

Castro stuffed his wallet in his back pocket and held out his hand for his phone. I gave it to him, got up, and wrapped my arms around his torso. As he'd been doing since he'd started showing cold symptoms, he avoided a kiss.

"You're over it," I said into his shoulder.

"Maybe." He returned the hug and whispered in my ear. "Just for today, to be safe. Tomorrow, watch out, pretty lady!"

I held on a moment longer, savoring the smell of his freshly-washed hair. "I'll remember that."

He gave me his signature goofy lopsided smile as he let me go. "I'll make sure of it." He left the apartment; Petunia watched him go, then headed into her box for a day-long nap.

5

It didn't take long for my phone to charge. As soon as it was ready, I stuffed it in my pants pocket, grabbed my keys, and was out the door.

The day was sultry and mostly sunny. Puffy white cotton ball clouds danced lazily over the city, not seeming to be in any particular hurry to get anywhere. Maybe that meant we'd have calm weather for a while. That would be nice. I loved sunny days, when the world seemed to half-sleep, half-stumble through the hours, though I could do without St. Louis' standard summertime humidity level of "tropical rainforest."

When I'm restless, I walk or drive without a destination in mind. Today was too hot to do much walking, so I got in Nixie and pottered around the city for a while. After a half-hour or so, I realized my destination was the location of the murder that had Castro so interested.

The location wasn't conducive to parking, so I found a meter a few blocks from the site and walked under the blazing sun the rest of the way.

The scene was no different than any other I'd seen walking here. Brick buildings radiated the heat of the day back into the atmosphere, as did the black asphalt street. Dumpsters crowded narrow alleys and lent the thick wet atmosphere a blanket of nasty odors you could cut with a knife. A few ants crawled along the pavement, marching in between bare sprigs of spindly weeds that took advantage of every crack in the sidewalk, but otherwise, the area was bare of life.

Why would Kendall have been here?

I strolled down the alley where he'd died, for no better reason than morbid curiosity. If there had ever been bloodstains or police tape in the area, they'd been removed. This alley looked like a million others. Nothing special about it. Nothing to show why anyone would come here, or why anyone would kill here.

And kill for what—a handful of keys? That made no sense.

I turned back toward my car, already weary from the pressure of the sunlight on my head and shoulders. At this time of year, the sun seemed to push you down, exerting a force that bent you over and crushed you under its merciless thumb. I had no doubt I was three inches shorter than usual just from the relentless rays of the sun.

Something glinted on the pavement in front of me. Change? I always picked up change when I found it lying around, even pennies. It was a habit Andre liked to goad me about, but pennies spend as well as any other piece of currency.

I walked over but had only gone a step or two when my heart stopped and the blood in my veins turned to ice water. The object was a key.

The key.

I backed away but from behind me came a scraping sound. I swiveled around, hands up, ready to hit something, anything, if it meant escaping this crazy alley.

The alley contained nothing but Dumpsters.

And sobbing.

I hadn't believed my blood could get colder, but it did. I backed up, unwilling to turn my back on whatever invisible sobbing presence was in the alley with me.

A young man stepped out from behind a Dumpster. I'd never seen a more miserable looking individual in my life, not even in the darkest, scariest bars. In the bright light of day, somehow, his scruffy clothes and tear-stained face were even more tragic. He had medium-colored skin and his hair was too short to be an afro, but longer than many guys wore it nowadays. His face was covered in tears.

"Who are you?" I was glad I had enough voice to make myself heard and didn't squeak.

He reached for me with blood-stained hands, and, as if a switch had been flipped in my head, I suddenly felt the strangest craving. I wanted to touch him. While a small voice in the back of my mind screamed *run, you idiot!* the rest of me took a step forward. Something about this young man called to me. He was lost and alone and...

...dead. He was dead. Why did that not bother me? I reached for him, and the young man's expression went from grief-stricken to terrified. He backed up. *He feared me.*

The new alarming hunger inside me gloried in that fear. Reveled in it. It was so unlike a hunger for food or sex. It was wretched and secret and overpowering like nothing else had ever been. And it was insatiable. Without even being conscious of making the decision to move, I darted forward and grabbed at the image of Marco Kendall. Grabbed at a dead man.

He was no match for me. I wrapped my arms around him in a hideous embrace and squeezed. My skin pricked all over as if small creatures were crawling on me. Coldness seeped through my pores and settled into the very core of my being. I filled up on the chill, completely shutting out the heat of the day and the weight of the sunlight. I could have stood there all day soaking up that strange frostiness, letting it settle into the farthest corners of my soul.

"Teryl?" someone shouted.

I opened my eyes and stumbled forward, suddenly conscious again of the heat. I caught myself from falling and leaned against the nearest Dumpster. Nausea surged up my gut and I puked. Gut muscles clenched over and over until I had nothing more to vomit onto the asphalt. A horrible loneliness wrapped itself around my chest and compressed my heart, and a tiny voice in my head was screaming at me for being so stupid as to run toward a specter instead of away from it.

Someone ran up behind me. "Teryl, what happened? Are you okay?" It was Fish. He placed a hand on my shoulder and the nausea retreated a smidgen. I wasn't alone.

Slowly, I pulled myself together. Fish, uncharacteristically quiet, gave me the time and did nothing more than keep a hand on me. After several minutes, I stood up straight. Fish handed me a cloth. I didn't ask where it came from or how clean it was, I just wiped my mouth on it. I gave it back to Fish and he tossed it in the Dumpster.

"I'm going insane," I said.

"No," said Fish almost immediately. "You're not. It's George."

"Will you stop with the fucking George shit!" I shouted. I pushed Fish away and stumbled toward my car. "This is crazy. I just hugged a dead guy. I don't even want to know why I didn't do the sane thing and run away."

"What's crazy? What's insane?" asked Fish. "A guy died here. You saw him. Maybe it was just the power of suggestion."

"That was no fucking *suggestion*. And I thought you were all about quantum physics or some shit."

Fish walked beside me and patted me awkwardly on the arm. I got the feeling he wasn't used to being on the giving end of sympathy, or at least he hadn't been for a long time. "You're lost,

Teryl. I can't explain it any better than that, except to say that it's George. It's not you that's crazy. It's the world."

That was not exactly reassuring, coming from Fish. "I'm hallucinating," I said. "I'm going nuts. There's no other explanation."

"Just call it George."

A deep-seated anger flared in my chest and for a moment, I hated Fish for mocking me. "Stop talking about fucking George! There is no George!"

Fish held out his hands in a gesture of surrender. His brown eyes were sorrowful. In the bright sunlight, I saw that the irises were flecked with the same red that was in his hair. He suddenly looked more exotic and regal than he ever had in the bar. "Remember what I told you last night?" he asked earnestly. "George is shorthand for the weird shit the universe throws at us. He's not real, exactly. But the universe is a bizarre place. Unexplainable crap happens, and some places are more, well, afflicted, than others. Some people say those places are haunted, but that's as stupid as saying it's George. It's still shorthand for weird fucking shit that no one should have to see or hear or experience. I'm not saying what you saw and heard wasn't there. It simply wasn't...explainable."

"That's ridiculous."

He shrugged and put his hands down. "If you're going to work at the Angels' Share, you're going to have to get used to it. Some old places have a lot of, oh, call it *georgeness*, to them, and that's one of the places. You know, once Ware had a bartender start shrieking in the middle of his shift about dead faces in the corners. He *climbed over the bar* in a mad panic, and dashed out the door. Left his keys, his jacket, and even his wallet behind, and it was below zero that night. Don't know how he made it anywhere without freezing to death. Never came back for his things, either. Ware had a messenger take the stuff to the guy's apartment, but the guy never came near the building again."

I took a few moments to digest that while sweat trickled down my back and face. I wasn't sure I believed it; maybe Fish was trying to calm me down with a likely story. "You're there a lot. Do you see things?"

"No," he said. But that was so obvious a lie, he didn't even blink when I gave him a skeptical look. "All right, yes. Sometimes. But the amount of georgeness people experience varies."

"This isn't the Angels' Share," I said. "Even if what you say is true, shouldn't this stuff only happen at work?"

Fish sighed. "Who knows? Now, can you drive home?"

We had reached Nixie. Fish opened the driver's side door and said "oh."

I looked in the car. The key was there. *It had gotten itself from the bar to my apartment to the alley and now to my car.* I clapped my hands over my mouth to stifle a scream and sank to my knees on the hot asphalt. My head pounded in pain in time with my heartbeat and the nausea started to curl around my gut once more. "No, no, no," I said. "This can't be. It's following me. Get rid of it."

"I hate to say this, but that doesn't really appear to be an option," said Fish, his voice choked with concern. "But I'll take the key so you don't have to. And I'll drive you home. Okay?"

The asphalt was beginning to burn my knees. I pulled myself to my feet with some help from Fish and hoped the nausea would remain at bay. "Okay," I said at last.

"It's okay," said Fish. "Some rest, some water, and some time will set it all right."

Obviously, another lie, but I let it go. "All right."

Fish guided me around to the passenger side of the car and even helped me into the seat as if I were made of the most brittle porcelain.

Hell, for all I knew, I was.

6

All the way home, I fretted that introducing Fish to Castro was going to be a disaster. "Hi, honey, I'm home! And by the way, this is one of the sots that hangs out at the bar." That did not seem to be something that had a chance of going over well. "Oh, and I almost forgot—he wants me to believe in the supernatural, only he calls it George and hints that it's all about quantum mechanics or some other weird-ass crap."

Um...yeah.

But I underestimated Castro, or he'd been wanting to meet Fish after all my colorful stories about the regulars at the bar. He grinned widely when I stepped into the apartment, and said, "This must be Fish!" He stepped forward, hand out, which Fish took delicately, as if he couldn't quite believe he was welcome here.

"How did you know I was coming?" he asked.

Castro kept grinning that idiotic smile. "I didn't. But I've heard you described. Wouldn't have mistaken you for anyone else."

Fish nodded soberly. "Interesting." He gave me a strange look and I shrugged.

Castro noticed. "Hey, she only tells good stories."

Fish relaxed a little. "I'm on my best behavior at the bar. She should only have good stories to tell." He noticed Petunia. "Ah, you have a little friend I've never heard a word about."

"That's Petunia," said Castro proudly. "She's my best girl. Well, among insectivores."

"Hello, Petunia," said Fish. Petunia actually sniffed in his direction, even though midday was a time she was usually sacked out in her box. She came up to the bars of the cage, sniffed again, yawned, and retreated to her den.

"That's a better greeting than most get," said Castro. "I'd call that a hearty endorsement."

Again, it seemed Petunia liked others better than she liked me.

"Traitor," I said under my breath.

"So, Teryl kind of had an upsetting morning. Could we get her something to drink and some lunch?" asked Fish.

Castro was instantly at my side. "Upsetting? Did you get mugged? Carjacked?"

I shook my head and leaned on him. He wrapped his arms around me and the world was suddenly a helluva lot better than it had been two seconds before.

"I don't even know what happened. It's like I'm going crazy," I said.

Castro hugged me more tightly. "Sit down. I'll get you some water and then make lunch. What sounds good to you—a BLT on wheat? Tuna salad on rye? Eggs and bacon?"

"Whatever," I said as I sank onto the couch.

Castro looked over at Fish. "You have a preference?"

Fish shuffled his feet, appearing uneasy and embarrassed. "Honestly, anything would be great. You don't have to cater to me."

"Nonsense," said Castro. "If you want it, and I can make it, it's yours."

My heart swelled with pride and affection for this man. His dedication to being a good, no, a *great*, host, was genuine and was one of the ways he'd won my heart. Castro said he'd never felt welcome in any of the foster homes he'd lived in, and if it were up to him, no one who stepped into his home would ever feel that way if he could help it. And he always followed through on that. I should have known he would be the perfect host; it was just that I'd never thought I'd be bringing Fish home.

I'd never thought I'd be bringing Fish home on a morning when I hugged a specter and got haunted—again—by a key.

"Ah, then the BLT sounds great," said Fish. He actually flushed a little. I wondered how long it had been since someone had made him a meal.

"Have a seat on the couch," said Castro. "Petunia's occupying the only table we have, so you'll have to balance your plate on your lap, but otherwise, we can be civilized here."

"Civilized," said Fish with a hint of wistfulness. "Doesn't that sound grand?"

I had no idea what he meant by that, but then, this was Fish, the guy that claimed to be an ex-sponge diver-turned gigolo.

Fish left Petunia's cage with seeming reluctance. Maybe he really liked animals or something. I'd never heard stories about animals in all his tales. Much like where he lived, where he got the money to pay for alcohol, and how he'd ended up at the Angels' Share, most of Fish was still a mystery to me.

Up to now, that's how I preferred it. But as he gingerly sat on the couch, as if he didn't trust it to hold his weight, I got the overwhelming feeling that the stuff he was hiding was much more interesting than I could guess. And that one day, if I listened long enough, I'd hear all about it.

That thought did not make me happy.

7

The BLTs were delicious, of course, since Castro made them rather than me. I could barely warm up a hot dog properly, and I'd always thought those things were both bad for you and idiot-proof. But even more than that, the care with which he attended to both me and Fish made me realize all over again how lucky I was to have this guy in my life. Right now, nothing could have convinced me to let him go. Not for the world.

Castro made sure everyone was served and had a drink before sitting in our only chair. Fish and I were on the couch. I had recovered enough to be embarrassed by the frayed nature of its brown canvas upholstery, but as long as it still held people off the floor, I wasn't spending money on a new one.

"So, did you run into each other at the bar?" he asked. "I thought Teryl's shift didn't start until five."

"It does," I said around a bite of BLT.

"No," said Fish at almost the same time. "We didn't meet at Angels' Share. At least, not this morning. I was wandering around and happened to spot her in an alley."

I swallowed the bite of sandwich I had been chewing. "I read those news stories you had on your phone, about the guy who was murdered near the bar. So I was driving around and sorta ended up there."

"Huh," said Castro. He turned to Fish. "She's usually not into the weird stuff. That's my weakness. The weirder the news, the more I want to read about it."

Fish cocked his head. "I find it fascinating myself, but it's probably wiser to stay away from most of it. You never know what might be out there."

"Yet you hang out at the bar you claim has georgeness," I said. "That's hardly staying away." At Castro's questioning look, I said, "Fish's word for a place that seems haunted or otherwise has odd things going on."

"It's a comfortable place to hang out."

That seemed patently untrue. Bars like the Angels' Share, where we didn't serve food, didn't have live music, and didn't care if clients lit up a cigarette, were not places best described by the word *comfort*. They were places to go to get drunk. Places designed to help you forget whatever wretched hell your personal life had devolved into. You didn't go there for a bachelor party or a twenty-first birthday celebration. You went there to get shitfaced if you were lucky, and to stare vacantly into your drink as you ruminated on the ruin of your life if you weren't.

"The bar is haunted?" asked Castro. He practically twitched in excitement. "You never told me that!"

"It's not haunted," I said.

Fish rolled his eyes and sighed dramatically.

"Okay, weird things sometimes happen, but that's not necessarily the same thing," I said. "And stop with the eye rolling. It's unbecoming on someone your age."

Fish blinked in surprise but visibly wilted. I instantly regretted my outburst, though I had no idea why it had upset him.

"Did someone die there? Is it an old jail or something? Satanist hideout?" asked Castro.

"No," said Fish slowly. I had the odd feeling he was measuring his words carefully. "At least, I don't think anyone was ever jailed there."

"Why would you even know if someone had?" I asked.

"I've been hanging out there for years. You've only been there four months."

"So what odd things are going on?" asked Castro. "Is that key part of it?"

Fish startled. "The key again?"

"It showed up here last night." I shrugged, trying my best to appear as if this weren't freaking me out, and looked over at Castro. "While I was at the crime scene, it appeared twice. First on the asphalt, and then later in my car." I closed my mouth before I could mention seeing a dead guy and wrapping my arms around him, and soaking up...something cold. Something unexplainable. I didn't want to think about that, much less talk about it.

"Whoa." Castro's mouth literally hung open for a few moments. "Where is the key now?"

Fish drew it out of a pocket and held it in the palm of his hand. Castro stared at it with a kind of hunger in his eyes. As if all his investigations of weirdness were now nothing compared to being in the same room with it. He could stop living vicariously and experience the real thing up close and personal.

"I think Teryl should find out what this goes to," said Fish. He put the key down on the arm of the couch. "Otherwise, I think it will keep showing up."

That annoyed me. "Look, I'm not going to pay attention to this thing. Bizarre shit happening around me is not my life. I refuse to make it my life. Throw that fucking key out and forget about it."

"You tried that last night," said Fish apologetically. "And then it followed you home, and then to the alley."

Castro's nostrils flared, which I swear I thought only happened in books. "This is epic! What are you going to do to find out what it means?"

"I'm not doing anything." I stood up and took my plate to the kitchen to keep the men from seeing how jumpy this was making me. "And I'm not talking about this anymore." I kept the remainder of my sandwich, went to the bedroom, and slammed the door behind me, regretting ever letting Fish into my car, let alone my home.

I finished the sandwich while the men spoke in the other room. I heard the muted sound of their voices, but they did not speak loudly enough for me to hear. That was fine with me. Castro could talk about aliens or Bigfoot or the chupacabra for hours if he found an interested ear to bend.

Fish, it seemed, was interested, despite his protestations that it was best to avoid the topic.

I couldn't puzzle it out. Fish didn't have to hang out at the Angels' Share. Seedy bars were hardly an endangered species, and he didn't exactly seem close to any of the other regulars. He wasn't part of Ware's inner circle. But maybe he believed every place like the Angels' Share had georgeness, so it didn't matter which one he went to. Maybe it was the closest to where he lived.

Wherever that was.

Someone rapped on the door.

"Hey, Teryl," said Castro. "We're going back to the alley and then see if we can talk to the guy's girlfriend."

I opened the door. Castro looked eager to have a plan for the afternoon. I heard Fish mumbling something to Petunia that sounded like, "hey, sweetie, cute little thing." Wouldn't necessarily have pegged him for an animal person. But then, I never had been, either. Maybe it was just Petunia.

What Castro said finally sank in. "You want to, what, chase down the guy's girlfriend and interrogate her about her recently shot-to-death boyfriend? Isn't that a bit ghoulish, if not downright stalkerish?"

Castro opened his mouth, then closed it, and appeared to consider. But his body almost hummed in excitement; he was like a bowstring pulled back and ready to go. After a week of inactivity, he had energy to burn, and this coincided with his fascination with the supernatural. He wasn't going to consider what I'd said for long.

"Maybe. But we'll take pains to look harmless."

I snorted. "Trust me, two unidentified men walking up to your door and knocking on it does not appear harmless, even when they have on white shirts and black pants and you know they're Mormon kids handing out literature."

Men *do not get it*. Women think about their personal safety before they open a door or walk down a street. Men never do.

"Come with us," said Castro. He gestured vaguely toward the front door. "Then maybe we won't look dangerous."

I wasn't sure which was more annoying, the assumption that my presence might defuse a tense introduction, or the idea that he might be right. Still, I had no intentions of bothering a grieving woman about her recently-deceased loved one.

"No way," I said. "I am not bothering this woman. And if you can honestly understand that *two* people could look dangerous, what would *three* people look like, even if one of them is a woman?"

"Okay," he said, without bothering to think about it. Big surprise. "Well, we're going. We'll let you know how it goes." He gave me a peck on the cheek and headed toward the door.

"Not interested in knowing that," I called out after him.

"You probably will be," said Fish. He did not sound excited at the prospect. Why was he going if he wasn't interested? I swear, I did not understand one thing about the man.

The door closed behind them and I sat down on the bed. I could not see how this little adventure could possibly pan out. Even if the woman did agree to talk to them, what would she know about a key hidden in her boyfriend's wallet?

The key. Fish had it. What if he produced it? Wouldn't the woman assume he'd somehow stolen it from the police and call them? Or perhaps Fish would have more sense than to show it to her.

Maybe it wouldn't be in his pocket once they got there.

I shuddered. I had no idea why this key kept appearing and disappearing and didn't want to know. But I had an awful gut feeling that, eventually, I would be forced to find out.

8

I left for work around half past four in the afternoon, and Castro had not returned. Well, maybe he and Fish had decided to head to the bar after their crazy day of stalking grieving girlfriends on a ridiculous quest to discover information about a key that refused to stay in one place, despite all physical laws to the contrary.

I was glad I had not gone with them. I tossed Petunia a few dried mealworms, which she nosed delicately, and headed out.

The bar was nearly deserted, no surprise for a Thursday. A couple sat in one of the booths on the far wall, near Ware's office. They were dressed in jeans and tees, and looked more like they were students at the university a few miles away, so I assumed they were slumming in this neighborhood and probably wouldn't become regulars. But you never knew.

Jeff was the daytime bartender. His short blond hair, thousand watt smile, and surfer body made him seem out of place in a dark smoky bar a thousand miles from the ocean, but he was actually from the area and had never wanted to go anywhere else. He waved at me, and made a show of getting out his car keys. "Glad you're here a few minutes early. Got plans!"

"What are they this time?" I asked as I walked behind the bar. I could see that Jeff had everything set up ready to go. I had learned, in the six weeks he'd been here, that while he might be flaky in other areas of his life, Jeff was an excellent bartender.

The "plans" that Jeff always had were part of his flakiness, which, for some reason, I found adorable. Maybe because Jeff never seemed upset when things didn't work out the way he'd hoped. The girl he was sure was "the one" but who turned him down for a second date? He sighed and said "maybe the next one." The group of friends who were going to head out to a casino and play the slots until the wee hours and then who all decided to stay home and drink beer instead? He shrugged his shoulders and said "I like beer fine."

Someday, things were going to go Jeff's way. They had to. How could a guy that accommodating and attractive stay single?

His smile was as wide and brilliant as usual. "Going to a bachelor party. It's going to be wild. Like, really wild. Maybe with strippers, or even a trip to a topless bar."

"Okay," I said. "Have fun."

He leered at me. Well, he tried to. There was no way someone with Jeff's broad friendly face, steel gray eyes, and perfect white teeth could actually *leer*. "The hearts of my dollars are yours, gorgeous, even if they end up in a stripper's G-string. Don't get jealous."

I laughed. "Promise."

Someone else might have been insulted, but Jeff laughed, too. He waved and was out the door. I took another look around the bar to see if I'd missed anyone. But the couple in the booth were the only customers at the moment.

It was going to be a slow night, I was sure.

After twenty minutes, the couple were still chatting amiably in soft voices and I was getting bored. Jeff had clearly been bored, too, because the back of the bar was as neat as I'd ever seen it, with bottles lined up perfectly, and all the tools of the trade in their exact correct places. Dishes with lemon wedges and cherries were filled. I grabbed a cherry and ate it and contemplated if there were anything Jeff had left undone.

The door opened and I looked up, relieved at last to have someone to serve, and wondering if it might be Fish and Castro, back from their adventure.

The man who walked in was someone I had never seen before. He was tall, maybe six-and-a-half feet, and paler than Fish. He had off-white hair streaked with brown and dark eyes shaded by heavy brows. His eyebrows and five o'clock shadow were dark brown, so I assumed the hair color was the result of a bad dye job. He wore solid black, which made his skin look abnormally pale under the lights of the bar.

He walked to the bar slowly, economically, as if every move were orchestrated ahead of time. He slid onto a stool and put his elbows on the counter. "Whiskey."

People who don't tell you what kind of whiskey they want get whatever medium-quality stuff is almost to the bottom of the bottle. Serve something too expensive and they protest. Serve something really cheap and they protest even more. So pick something mid-range until the customer starts giving more specific details as to what they want. Today, as I surveyed the likely choices, it looked like "whiskey" meant a Speyburn 10-year.

The customer watched me pour the slightly peaty golden liquid into a shot glass and said nothing. He merely sipped it once I put it in front of him and nodded appreciatively.

Usually, I could chat with customers a bit to make them open their wallets more than they might otherwise. But I felt reluctant to speak with this man. It wasn't that he was covered in tattoos that said things like I KILL FOR FUN or anything like that. He simply sat at the bar like a force of nature, as if by measuring his steps and sitting down carefully, he had somehow found a way to bring something dangerous safely into the bar, and was now doing his best to control it.

Why he struck me that way I had no idea. I decided to escape for a moment and walked over to the booth. The couple had fallen silent and were eyeing my new customer.

"Can I get you guys anything else?" I said as I gathered up their empty beer glasses.

"No," said the guy. The woman with him shook her head.

"Do you know that man?" she asked quietly.

"No. Do you?"

Both of them shook their heads. So he was simply making them nervous by his very presence. Well, he was making me nervous, too, so I could hardly blame them.

"We already paid the last bartender," said the woman.

I nodded. Jeff would have told me if there were a tab open.

"Sure," I said. "Hope we see you again."

The woman gave me a wan smile, but then the two of them walked out as quickly as they could without looking back at my remaining customer.

I put the dirty glasses in the dishwasher and went back to wipe up the booth. I lingered a little longer than usual, to get a few extra seconds away from the bar. But I couldn't stand across the room forever when there was no obvious reason to avoid returning to my station.

After all, this was my job. I slapped a smile on my face and went back behind the bar. The man finished his whiskey and shoved the glass across the bar toward me. "Another."

"Sure thing," I said. I poured more Speyburn in the glass and the man began sipping his second shot. "Haven't seen you in here before," I said, the standard bartender opener. Safe enough. "You from around here?"

The man didn't take his eyes off his drink. "Nope."

"Well, I'm Teryl, if you need anything."

That made him look up. His eyes were so dark brown they might as well be black, and the black pupils sat in their milky white corneas almost like the pips on a die. I was immediately reminded of rolling snake eyes, and did not like the thought.

"Teryl," he repeated slowly. "Why?"

"Why what?"

"Why that name?"

Everyone wanted to know that, it was that most people said something like "Unusual name. What's it mean?" or "Pretty name; never heard it before." Not a bare "why?"

"My mother wanted to name me Sheryl," I said. I'd answered this question my whole life and had the spiel down pat. It was even true. "But my aunt named *her* daughter Sheryl, so my mother changed the first letter. I could have been Carol or Meryl or Beryl, I suppose, but Teryl was what she decided on."

"Better than Darrell, anyway," said the guy. He pulled his lips back in the craziest, most intimidating expression I'd ever seen. You'd be hard-pressed to say it actually was a grin, and you'd certainly never call it a smile.

"I guess so," I said, and tried a grin of my own, but I bet it was coming off more as a grimace. "Never thought about that particular name before."

"Pellagrio," he said.

"What?"

"My name."

"Oh. Well, nice to meet you," I said as sincerely as possible, which, at the moment, wasn't terribly sincere.

He glanced at the wall of bottles behind me. "Give me the Elijah Craig 12-year small batch, unless it's one of their new ones, then more of the Speyburn."

"Sure thing." I got another glass and grabbed the Elijah Craig bottle. The distillery had recently made the decision to mix 8-year and 12-year bourbons into their small batch, a decision that Pellagrio clearly didn't agree with. But this bottle was the old-style 12-year. It was nearly full; not many wanted to pay for it, even though it wasn't nearly the most expensive stuff in the house. Ware had a bottle of 30-year Highland Park in the back that I had only glimpsed once, and if there were anything even pricier in the building, he'd kept it to himself. The most expensive stuff out on the bar was a 21-year Bushmill.

"Leave the bottle."

I put the bottle down in front of him and he grabbed that and the glass and made his way to a booth.

Ware would be happy to see this guy's bar tab.

I wiped down the bar, and checked the time. Not quite six o'clock, which was normally when Fish came in. I leaned against the bar and waited while Pellagrio sucked down the Elijah Craig in his booth.

Six o'clock came and went, as did six thirty. I was screaming inside with boredom. Pellagrio had almost finished the bottle and I wondered if he'd have the constitution to stand up and walk back to the bar, or if he'd slide down onto the booth's upholstery and lie around a while.

By seven o'clock, Pellagrio was finished with the bottle and remained seated at the booth, staring at his empty glass. I pulled out my phone, despite the fact Ware didn't approve of employees making personal calls at work, and called Castro. Maybe he could tell me what had happened to Fish.

The call went to voicemail.

We didn't have a landline in the apartment, so if Castro didn't answer his phone, I had no way to reach him. I switched to texting.

How'd it go? Where are you?

Castro could usually be counted on to answer a text within five to ten minutes. But the minutes ticked by.

I put the phone away and bit my lip. It wasn't like Castro to not return calls or texts. At least, not when they were from me. Sometimes he'd return a call from Andre, and sometimes not, depending on how well or poorly Andre's last crashing-on-our-couch session had gone.

But he didn't leave *me* hanging.

By the time another ten minutes had passed, I had nearly convinced myself he'd had a car accident and was lying in a hospital bleeding to death, but after a couple more minutes, I had managed to convince myself he'd somehow lost his phone or had accidentally turned it off.

Not that he'd ever done that before, but *I* had, so I could imagine it happening.

Pellagrio got up from the booth and brought glass and empty bottle back to the bar. He walked as deliberately and carefully as he had last time, as if he'd been drinking water and not 94 proof bourbon.

"Decent stuff," he said as he placed the bottle and glass on the bar in front of me. His eyes wandered over the selection again.

"You know, it might be time to take a break," I said. My heart pounded as I said the words. I did not want to confront this man or deny him anything he asked of me. My knees shook.

His gaze left the wall behind me and drilled into me. The snake-eye glare was impossible to look away from. "Do I seem impaired to you?" he asked.

"Well, um, no," I mumbled. "No, you don't."

"Then I'll keep drinking."

I opened my mouth but nothing came out. I simply stared dumbly at Pellagrio, helpless to break eye contact.

"Did you hear me, bitch," he snarled. "More whiskey." He leaned forward and his hand snaked toward me as if to grab me by the throat.

I stumbled backward. At the same moment, the door to Ware's private office burst open and Ware exploded out of the back. Though he was shorter and older than Pellagrio, he was barrel-chested and strong as an ox and red-faced with anger. Ware hauled

Pellagrio off his bar stool and backed him across the room and up against the wall.

"Don't mess with my bartender," he hissed. "And you won't ever call her that name again, do you hear?"

"Or what?" asked Pellagrio. He seemed defiant, and I could see why. Ware was strong, sure, but how could he be a real threat to the younger man?

"You're not even worth threatening," said Ware. "And we both know who will win any fight." He shoved Pellagrio against the wall again.

The taller man hesitated, then made that grimace-grin again. "Sure."

Ware practically tossed the man back toward the bar. "Now pay her what you owe and get out. Next time I see you, be sure you've brought your manners with you."

Pellagrio didn't say anything to that, or even look at Ware. He pulled out a wad of bills from his back pocket and casually laid them on the bar. Before I could reach for them, he turned and walked out with that deliberate stride under Ware's withering stare.

When Pellagrio had gone, Ware came over. "You okay?"

"Sure," I said, though the tremor in my voice betrayed me.

Ware slid the bills toward me. I stared at the pile, then numbly began counting. Ware laid a hand on mine. His hand was cool and dry. The confrontation with Pellagrio didn't seem to have him in a cold sweat.

"No," he said. "They're yours. You earned them. I don't want his money, anyway."

"But the whiskey..."

"I'm not discussing this any further. The money's yours." He looked around the bar. "Where's Fish? He's usually here by now."

"I don't know. He and the guy I live with went out this afternoon and I haven't heard from them since." The story started to flow out of me, like an adrenaline-fueled confession. "There's this key that keeps showing up and Fish thinks it has something to do with this guy that got killed near here. I didn't want anything to do with it, but him and Castro, they left after lunch to go to the crime scene and to find this guy's girlfriend. I have no idea what they thought they could learn or why Castro hasn't called me or why Fish isn't here."

Ware tapped his fingers on the bar as if considering my words.

"Fish says weird things happen here all the time and another bartender went crazy because there were dead faces in the corners, and I don't know what to do, because I think I'm starting to go crazy, too. Last night, my rag was there and then not there and then there again. And then this key thing...but that's not even the worst."

I choked, not sure I could go on. I didn't want to talk about the alley. I'd avoided thinking about it for hours. But the vision of Kendall's terrified face wouldn't leave my mind once I recalled it.

Ware patted my hand again. "The worst?"

For some reason, that reassured me. I could tell Ware. He would understand.

"I went to the crime scene and saw the guy. *I saw him, like, literally standing there.* Like he was a real person and not dead for two weeks! And then I...I didn't run away like a normal person would. I grabbed hold of him and I felt him seeping into me. Or through me. Or something. I don't even know what happened. I don't want to think about it."

I gulped and finally stopped the flow.

Ware appeared to be seriously thinking about what to say. Throughout the bar, the air grew heavy and cold, and seemed to shimmer slightly as if ice crystals were suddenly everywhere. The weight on my chest was as bad as St. Louis on its worst day, when you felt like you were being crushed by the very atmosphere that normally supported you. I wanted to hear Ware say something ordinary, but something in my gut warned me not to get my hopes up. The rabbit hole was opening up beneath my feet and who knew where the bottom might be?

"Weird things do happen around here," said Ware at last. "Fish and Pellagrio and dead faces in corners and disappearing rags are hardly the extent of it."

Oh, fuck. Should I be like the last bartender and throw myself over the bar and run out? I was at a loss.

"I don't have any comforting things to say." Ware said with some sadness. "I think things are only going to get more intense from here on out. There's a fight coming but it's not your fight. Or your lover's. Anytime you want to leave, you can, at least as far as I'm concerned. Others might not be so magnanimous."

"Like Pellagrio?" I couldn't believe I said that. Surely the only good response to "there's a fight coming and it's not your fight so you can go" is "good-bye."

He shrugged. "Maybe. He was trying to scare you tonight. But he can be dangerous. Still, there are others more dangerous than he."

"If I leave, will they go away?"

Ware opened his mouth, then closed it. He sighed. "I don't think so. You're lost, Teryl. They know that. You say you didn't run away like a normal person, and that's more right than you know. You're not a normal person. You can see what others can't, and you can do things others could only dream of. But the cost is high. That's why it has to be your choice whether to stay or run."

My phone buzzed. I pulled it out of my pocket, glad to have something to do besides look at Ware. His last statement hung in the air between us: *your choice to stay or run.* Running would be the better option, surely, especially after that bizarre speech.

The phone had a received a text. *Come see what is found.*

"What the hell?"

Ware glanced at the text. He frowned. "Is that the kind of text you normally get from this guy—Castro?"

"No," I said slowly. "It doesn't sound like him." Hell, Castro could hardly be bothered to use any punctuation or capital letters, let alone archaic grammar like *see what is found.* Castro would have typed *com c wht I found* if he'd even bothered with *that* many letters.

Ware hesitated. "I should probably keep you here, lock the door, and hope Fish can cope with whatever the two of them stumbled into. But the days when that guy could consistently get dressed by himself are long gone. Your friend is completely unprepared."

"Unprepared for what?"

Ware shook his head. "It's too hard to explain. Do you know where they were going exactly?"

"The crime scene. That's maybe eight blocks from here. And then the girlfriend's house. I have no idea where that is."

"That paper last night that Fish was reading, you mean that murder?" At my nod, he continued, "I'm sure a search of the internet will bring up the address you need."

"I need the address?"

"You do if you want to find out what those two have gotten themselves into."

"Oh."

Gotten themselves into? Good God, the whole world was going crazy. How could a stupid lunch of BLTs and a lover with a penchant for weird news stories turn into something serious?

"You'll need something for protection," said Ware. "I'll be back."

"I don't know how to shoot," I called after him.

"Guns aren't likely to be of much use."

"Oh," I said quietly to myself.

Maybe it would be best to go with the crazy, since it seemed I was the only one even trying to hold onto sanity.

9

Ware emerged from his office a couple of minutes later and handed me a piece of paper with an address scrawled on it in old fashioned slanted letters like they used on the Declaration of Independence. I'd seen his handwriting before, and had always wondered why he'd cultivated such an archaic style. Everybody has to have a hobby, I guess.

"This is the place," he said. "Now, give me your hand."

I stared at him dumbly.

"Hand. Now." He held out one of his.

I put out my right hand and he turned it palm up. In his other hand he held a black marker. With several deliberate strokes, he drew some kind of symbol on my palm. It looked like a circle crossed with a few zigzags and short lines.

I stared at it.

"This might help," he said. "But I can't say how much. It depends on the situation and who's there."

Right. Because magic marker doodles are so very helpful in bad situations. But I could hardly say that to Ware when he seemed so sincere.

The door opened and I looked up quickly, a little embarrassed to be hand-in-hand with my boss. Still, if it were Fish and Castro, who cared if explanations were needed? I needed to know they were safe.

The woman who came in was willowy, blond, and dressed to the nines. A cloud of musky perfume accompanied her and almost made me sneeze. She said nothing but raised an eyebrow at Ware, who jerked his head toward his office door. "In the back. Be with you in a minute."

The woman went through the door marked PRIVATE without even a glance in my direction. The scent of her perfume remained in the air, as if we needed proof she'd been here. Ware dropped my hand. "I'll handle things here," he said. "If it gets too busy for some reason, I'll see if Hayley can come in."

He walked toward his office, turned back briefly, and said, "Good luck," passed through the doorway, and closed the door. The note of finality in his voice sent a shudder down my spine. What in the hell was going on with Fish and Castro?

Or, more precisely, what did my boss *think* was going on? After all, he didn't really know any more than I did. For all either of us knew, the two were knocking back shots at a different bar, or Castro had invited Fish back to the apartment to wax poetic about what he fed Petunia.

I headed out the door at a walk, but once I got to the street, an inner feeling of urgency made me jog the rest of the way to my car. I reached it, panting, and got inside before taking a good look at the address.

Ware's odd attitude was catching. No matter how much I told myself nothing was wrong, my gut insisted on a darker conclusion. Castro had followed Fish into a situation that neither of them had counted on. They needed help, or Castro, at least, would have called.

The weird text was another indication, if I needed any, that it was time for action. I put the car in drive and headed toward the address on the slip of paper.

The GPS on my phone led me to a small, well-kept neighborhood north of Olive near the Loop. North of the infamous "Delmar Divide," one of the main geographical boundaries between black and white neighborhoods. St. Louis had always been a city where redlining had been practiced with a vengeance.

I drove up Pennsylvania until I found Julian and turned. The house I parked in front of was small, brick, and well-cared for. The lawn was perfectly mowed and the bushes trimmed. That didn't fit the stereotype of the area, but it was not the only house flourishing under such good care.

I walked up to the door and rang the bell. In a few moments, a short Hispanic woman opened the door. She did not open the screen door, which did not surprise me.

"Yes?"

"I'm sorry to bother you," I said, "but I'm looking for someone who might have been here earlier today. He and another man…"

"Two men, yes," said the woman. "They wanted to know about that damn stupid key in Marco's wallet. I sent them packing."

"Oh, okay," I said. "Sorry again. They wouldn't happen to have mentioned where they were going?"

"No," she said. "I didn't even let them in. That guy with the ragged ear was *scary*."

That guy with the ragged ear.

"A big guy with a torn-up ear?"

"Yes. I did not let them in."

What in the world were the two guys from the bar last night doing here?

"Sorry I can't help you," she said as she started to close the door.

"Wait," I said again. "Those aren't the two men I'm looking for. My friends are dark-haired, and tall, and one is Hispanic. I'm pretty sure the Hispanic guy was wearing a t-shirt with Einstein's face on it."

At least, I thought that was the t-shirt Castro had on when he left the apartment. It was one of his favorites. Under Einstein's face were the words *Imagination is more important than knowledge.*

I had no idea if Einstein ever really said that, but Castro liked to think he had.

The woman stared at me for several long seconds before a kind of dawning recognition crossed her face. "You know, you remind me..." she started to say. Then she shook her head as if clearing it of a memory. "Yes, I saw those men, too. They came by later. They seemed very sincere and interested in Marco as a person, you know? Not a news story."

"They were here? Did they say where they were going next?"

"No, but I did show them Marco's stuff."

"Marco's...stuff?" What could that mean?

The woman stared at me a few more moments, made a decision, then unlocked the screen door and held it open. "Here, I'll show you. Lately, Marco had gotten obsessed with something. I don't understand it. Your friends were intrigued; I think that tall guy knew more than he said."

I entered the house quickly to keep as many of the annoying flying insects out as possible, and followed the woman through the cramped but neatly-decorated house to the back room. The woman swung the door open and inside was a conspiracy theorist's wet dream. Articles, pictures, and newspaper clippings were tacked onto every wall. I could barely take it all in.

"Every time something bizarre happened, Marco had to document it," said the woman. Her voice caught and she wiped a tear away from her face. "Your tall friend said most of it was noise—nothing connected to a larger picture, he said. But a few things snagged his interest, one in particular. The other guy thought it was all interesting."

I scanned the confusing mass of information on the walls. It was oddly organized but also oddly familiar, as if I'd seen a picture of it, or something very like it, before. "Which one was the most interesting one?"

She pointed to a small article on the far wall. I walked over and read the headline.

Strange Lights Seen at Old Chain of Rocks Bridge.

I didn't know much about that bridge. A couple of teenagers had been killed there a long time ago, before I was born. I didn't know the details. Otherwise, the bridge was a mystery to me.

The other clippings and articles, which had been printed from online sources, were equally as odd. *Goat-man Seen in Soulard. Mermaid Washes up in the Landing. Jennings Home Rates Visit from Denver-based Ghostbusters. Psychic Moving Due to City's "Hellmouth."* I guess the author of that article hadn't put much credence in the hellmouth idea, or it wouldn't have rated the quotation marks.

Odd things, indeed. But Fish had picked out the article on the bridge over everything else.

"I guess they planned on going there," said the woman. "The shorter guy was excited about it, but the other guy didn't want to go. I heard them arguing about it all the way to their car."

None of this made sense. Going to the bridge was the only thing I could think of that might help. I didn't know how to get to the bridge, but that's what GPS was for.

I walked back to the front door. The woman followed me. On the way, I saw a photo of a young man with medium-dark skin, hair too short to be an afro, and a dazzling smile. He looked like he had the world by the tail and a bright future. I blanched. This was the crying man in the alley.

"Is that Marco?" I asked. My voice squeaked and the woman gave me an odd look.

She nodded and blinked back tears. She picked up the picture and stared at it. "He was a good guy, the best I ever knew. He didn't deserve what he got."

"I'm sure he didn't," I said for lack of anything more comforting to say. I was still unwilling to think about the events in the alley and regretted having spotted the photo.

"You remind me of him somehow," the woman said a little dreamily. "Like how you know someone's around even when you can't see them. But that...that's impossible." She put down the photo and pushed the dreaminess aside. "You should go now."

"Sure," I said. "Thanks for your help." I was itching to get out and put this house behind me. I didn't want to think about the specter in the alley. And I didn't want this kind of pall in my apartment, not ever. Castro had to be all right. He had to be.

"Be careful," the woman said. "Those other guys seemed serious about something. Your friends were more like Marco—people who like to read about, and talk about, odd things. Those other people, though? Something's wrong with them." She closed the door and I heard the deadbolt slide. She had locked the world out.

The cold note in her voice made me shiver. I walked slowly back to my car and did my best to put fear aside. I was going to find Castro and bring him home, whatever it took. Whatever the cost.

That reminded me of Ware's warning. *The cost will be high.*

I took a deep breath and got in the car. Fuck that. I was going to get Castro, and I'd fuck with anyone who got in my way. I plugged *Old Chain of Rocks Bridge* into my phone's map app. I had barely typed the words Old and Chain before the app popped up with my destination.

The directions seemed easy enough, though some of the twists through the neighborhood appeared to be pushing me back south, away from my destination. My phone gave a hiccup of a beep and the screen went black.

Hell, I'd charged it a few hours ago. Now my phone was crapping out on me, too? I couldn't win.

I was pretty sure I remembered the way, though. And as long as I kept going east and north, I ought to get to the bridge. In fact, if I could find the river, all I'd have to do is go north to the bridge. It seemed a good plan.

After a dozen more twists and turns, I ended up on Hall Street. I couldn't recall ever driving on it before. It appeared to be an endless string of industrial warehouses and factories, at least on the east side. To my left were dark areas where I spotted the occasional tombstone. I remembered that both Bellefontaine and Calvary cemeteries were on my way to the bridge. Good. I was on the right track.

The road was nearly deserted. I traveled past property after property secured behind chain link fences. Finally, the monotony of warehouses was interrupted by a storage facility. A huge lighted sign announced *We Stor 4 U.*

I don't know why they couldn't have kept the *e* in the word store, but whatever.

Something plopped in my lap. I jumped and swerved, heart pounding. Was someone throwing things at me? Was someone in the car with me? What in the hell was going on?

I pulled over, even though there was no proper shoulder and I was blocking half of the right lane. I had the steering wheel in a death grip and my nausea returned. Cold sweat trickled down my face and back. I looked down at my lap to see what had fallen into it.

It was the key.

"What do you want?" I screamed at it. Because screaming at inanimate objects was a productive thing to do. But I didn't care.

The key just lay there. It was so cold, I felt it through my jeans. As if it had just been in a freezer. It hadn't been like that before. I picked it up and put it in the passenger seat where it could be cold all it liked.

I looked back at the road. If I kept heading north, I should get to the bridge. But my brain refused to contemplate driving again. The key had come to me in *this place*. That had to mean something.

A car pulled up behind me. I tensed. It wasn't a police car, and this wasn't known for being a great neighborhood after dark. On the other hand, this person might merely be a Good Samaritan who saw someone on the side of the road and decided to see if they could help. I could always hope for that, anyway.

To my surprise, I recognized who got out of the car. It was the woman Ware and his friends called Little Girl.

Had Ware sent her after me? But he had no idea I'd be going toward the Old Chain of Rocks Bridge. Little Girl shouldn't have known my destination, either.

I rolled down the window as she sauntered up to the side of my car. She was so tall, she had to bend over to speak to me. She placed her right hand on the top of my car and smiled at me.

"Hi, Teryl," she said in her low voice.

"Hi."

"Having troubles?"

"Um..." I had nothing to say to that. Troubles? Was the right answer here to say yes? No? Thanks for stopping, but everything's all right? I had no idea how to respond. I'd never said more than "hello" to this woman before, and I couldn't recall that she'd ever said my name until now.

"I'll take that as a yes," she said. "Otherwise, why would you be out here after dark, pulled over, face looking stormy? Something's riding your heels, isn't it? Where you headed?"

I took a deep breath. No reason not to say. "The Old Chain of Rocks Bridge. I think Fish and my friend Castro went there."

Little Girl blinked, I swear in surprise.

"Now that's an odd place for Fish to go," she said. "Why there?"

"I don't know. The problem is this key." I pointed to it in the passenger seat. "It keeps appearing and disappearing. It appeared here, dropped right on my lap. I don't know what it means." My eyes were caught by the lighted billboard again. "Unless it goes to one of the storage units."

I gestured vaguely toward the storage lockers.

Little Girl came to attention suddenly, and her manner became much more serious. "Oh," she said.

"What?"

She hesitated, glanced back toward her car, and then tapped the roof with her long fingers. She seemed to come to some kind of decision.

"I see Ware sent you, that's all," she said.

I glanced at my hand with the odd marker scribble. "He didn't send me," I said. "But he did say this was protection."

"Hmm," said Little Girl. "That it is, under the right circumstances. So, why don't we team up and find out if that key goes to a storage locker?"

Her sudden desire to help me didn't make sense. She clearly had somewhere else to be. But perhaps Ware would want her to help me, much as he had Fish watching me when I walked out of the bar at night.

"They won't open for hours," I said. "So how will we find the right locker?"

"Oh, I have a way with locks and cameras," said the other woman. She strode toward the gate and studied it a few moments. "Bring the key!" she called back.

I was so going to jail tonight. But Little Girl was not someone you disobeyed lightly. Not that she'd threatened me, but she stood well over six feet and was muscled like an athlete. It was not difficult to imagine her with a javelin or sword, making her way across the battlefield, leaving a bloody mess in her wake. She was daunting without saying a thing, but once she had given a direct order, she was even more so.

Reluctantly, I picked up the key, got out of the car and walked up to the other woman as she slid the gate open. "Told you," she said.

She smiled again. Her white teeth shone in the night like stars. The rest of her was like a tall lithe pool of night: skin so dark it was almost blue, black clothing, and black hair cropped to a fraction of an inch so that every ridge and dip on her skull showed through. Only the teeth altered the monotony. I realized it was the first time I'd seen her without a dozen silver bracelets on each arm.

"Keep your hands on that key. Now, let's go," she said. "Pull your car in so no drunk hits it. I'll grab some things from my car and follow you in."

Wordlessly, I continued to obey. I pulled in just beyond the gate and parked to the side. I got out, slipped the key into my pocket, and waited for Little Girl to join me in the brightly lit lot.

In moments, she had her car next to mine and got out. She reached back in the car and grabbed a satchel, the kind that bike messengers carried, and slung it over her shoulder.

"Let's see this key."

I handed it over. She twiddled it between her fingers briefly and sighed. "Doesn't seem all that unusual. And there's no number on it. If it goes to a storage unit, shouldn't it have a number on it?"

"I don't know. I've never rented one."

"Fine. Let's go." She handed the key back to me and marched toward the nearest storage locker. She gestured toward the door. "Try it."

The key didn't fit. Not surprising. Even if the key did go to a storage locker, there had to be several thousand of them here. What were the odds that the key would fit the very first one I tried?

"Go on, try the next one."

Did Little Girl think we should try the key in *every* lock? That would take days. We'd be caught trespassing long before then. But I went to the next door as ordered, and once again met failure. After a dozen, I lost count, and Little Girl seemed to be losing interest. She began wandering around the facility, checking door handles and, I guess, assessing how many lockers there were to try.

I listened for sirens, but though the night was full of noises like the drone of cicadas and the hum of the overhead lamps, as well as the scrape of the key on the locks and my shoes trampling the pockmarked, deteriorating asphalt beneath my feet, traffic noise was almost nonexistent. I took a deep breath of the humid night air and wished I could just know where Castro was. I wanted to go home. I wanted to be at work. Anywhere except trespassing in the middle of the night with a freaking Amazon looking for I-don't-know-what by using a magical disappearing key.

How had this turned into my life?

I finished trying every door in one building. By this point, I was convinced the key didn't fit any of the lockers, and I wanted to leave. But I couldn't just bail. I did not think Little Girl would stand for that.

So...where was my companion?

"Hey!" I called out.

A tall slice of darkness slid around the corner of the next building. "You could just say my name."

I opened my mouth, but there was no way I could call this intimidating figure *Little Girl* out loud. Ware might be able to, but not me.

"I...I don't know it," I said at last.

She snorted. "Call me Babs."

Babs? Seriously? That wasn't going to come out any better than Little Girl.

She saw my face and realized that wasn't going to work. She sighed. "No? Fine. Try Oya. See if that's exotic enough for you."

"Okay...Oya." I got that out, but it still seemed too bare, too plain for the person who stood in front of me.

"So, what's up?" she asked. "I'm starting to think that key doesn't go to one of these lockers."

"Um, yeah, that's what I was thinking. Maybe I need to get back on the road. Get to the bridge."

She gave me an odd look. "I don't think you'll find what you're looking for there."

I opened my mouth, then closed it. I didn't have the brass to tell this woman she might be wrong. I might *think* it, but say it out loud? Not in this lifetime.

She crossed her arms. "Okay, what else is going on here, Teryl? You must know more or you wouldn't be heading for the bridge."

"What?" I could barely speak to this woman, and she thought I could withhold information or even lie to her? How was that even possible?

"Ware said there was something about you when he hired you. I wasn't sure, but I've never known him to be wrong about important things. Tequilas, maybe. But not *this*. Are you lost?"

Finally, a wave of anger pushed back my fear of this woman, just a little. That was the third time today someone had referred to me as *lost*.

"I don't know what the fuck you're going on about," I said. "I'm worried about Castro. Not you, not Ware. I don't know what your little club talks about after I leave work, but if it's me, I don't appreciate it. I expect Fish to say outrageous things for me to laugh at and pretend to believe. But I'd thought Ware, and maybe you, weren't into that. Now piss off while I go back to my car, try to find Castro, and hope I don't get arrested before morning for this stupid stunt."

In anger, I raised my hand and, to my amazement, Little Girl backed off. I swear there was fear in her eyes for just a moment.

"Sorry," she said. "I thought...well, never mind what I thought. I'm sorry, Teryl. Truly."

I lowered my hand. To my amazement, she sounded sincere and she cast her eyes down toward her feet. I thought she might really be sorry.

For what, though, I couldn't quite fathom. She seemed much more remorseful than someone who'd done what she had. I mean, sure, she'd basically accused me of holding out on her, but being sorry for *that* wouldn't rate the genuine sadness she appeared to be feeling.

I couldn't worry about it. It probably had something to do with her and Ware, anyway, and I didn't care.

A bright pink flash illuminated the area for a split second, making me jump. My heart nearly stopped. The police!

But my rational mind took over immediately. The police wouldn't be flashing anything *pink*. Whatever was going on, they still weren't involved.

I blinked back the afterimage and looked around. A faint glow stood out to my left, across the road. A curious sound seemed to emanate from it, a low hum that tickled my ears and stomach and rattled my teeth. For a moment, I felt lightheaded and was unsure I'd remain standing. I teetered, but for the moment, I was still up. I scratched at an ear but the obnoxious sound continued to turn my body annoyingly against me.

"I think we know where we need to go next," my companion said.

The darkness beyond the road was absolute. No street lights, no house lights, nothing. It was like a hole in the world.

The cemetery.

11

"Well," said Little Girl. "Things become clearer."

"They do?"

She clapped me on the shoulder. If the sound were affecting her like it was me, she was keeping the effects well-hidden. "Sure. Bet there's a fence over there somewhere, and the fence will have a gate, and that key will work in it. Let's go see if I'm right."

I shook my head slowly, hoping the dizziness would pass soon. "Trespassing twice in one night? Why are we doing this?"

"You saw the light. Something's going on over there. You should find out what it is."

"I should? Why don't you go by yourself?" I was caught between anger and fear. Fear of the cemetery. Fear of Little Girl. Fear, even, of returning to Ware without answers about Fish. And, somehow, fear that something was going on that I'd better understand, sooner rather than later, before I got in too deep to get out.

But above all, fear for Castro. I couldn't even contemplate my apartment with just me and Petunia. For a moment, I imagined her sniffling at her food bowl, wondering why it was me rather than Castro putting her cat food in it.

That was stupid. A stupid thought. But it shot a bolt of grief through me. I could not go home without Castro, and not just because Petunia would miss him.

I didn't want to live without him. Why hadn't that been obvious to me before? Why was the possibility of losing something the moment you realized how tightly you had to hold on to it?

The other woman began striding away without answering. Reluctantly, I followed, slightly unsteadily, and walked past Nixie with only one despairing glance in her direction. *Don't get towed while I'm gone!*

I could well imagine the car might tell me *Don't get arrested; I don't want to go to impound.*

"Oya," I said, still uncomfortable addressing her as anything at all.

"Yes?"

"What's really going on here? You seem to know." My teeth still felt as if they were being slowly shaken out of my skull. I wanted nothing more than to grit them together to keep them in my head.

The woman walked straight across Hall Street without looking left or right. I double-checked that there was no traffic and scuttled after her. "Well?"

She nodded but her attention was focused up the hill. "I have a good idea. The meat of it is, there are people who want to do bad things to other people. We can stand back and let them do it, or we can try to stop them."

"Isn't that what the police are for? Or the army?"

That earned me a frown. "You can feel the power coming down off this hill, can't you? Do you really think any army could cope with it?"

"I don't know," I said despairingly as Oya began running her hands over the wrought iron fence that surrounded the cemetery. "They'd be better equipped than *me*."

"One would think. Now, look for a fucking gate, why don't you?"

Helpless to disobey, I began searching. It only took a couple of minutes to find a gate. I felt for a lock. A sinking feeling crossed my mind that Oya had been right. The key probably went to *this*. I was about to open the gate into a dark cemetery in the middle of the night, while "people who want to do bad things to other people" were doing something inside.

This had all the hallmarks of a very, very bad idea. And yet, I was determined to move forward if it put me closer to Castro. If he were one of the people bad things would happen to, then there was nowhere else for me to be.

I slipped the key into the lock. It did not turn. Relief flooded through me. "It doesn't work." I pocketed the key again.

My companion grunted. "Well, as I said, I *do* have a way with locks." She placed her hands on the lock and rattled it back and forth a few times. Within moments, a snapping sound filled the air and the gate swung open.

"After you."

Dread made my feet feel as if they were encased in concrete and I did not care. I stepped over the line of the fence and into the cemetery. I turned back in time to see Oya elbow the satchel she carried. I heard a grunt and the satchel twitched.

She had something alive in the satchel. A puppy? Kitten? Ferret? Whatever it was, it couldn't be very big.

Oya saw the direction of my gaze. "Nothing to worry about. Thresholds can be...tricky sometimes." Moonlight glinted off her fabulously white teeth as she smiled and stepped into the cemetery. That caused the satchel to grunt again, but Oya ignored it. "They always complain at first. Now, up the hill!"

I swallowed my horror—what was I going to do, wrestle this woman for the satchel, miraculously win, and then let whatever-it-was go in the dark? The best I could do was concentrate on the task at hand, and worry about other things later. One thing at a time. That was the only way to get through.

Oya strode up the steep slope as if it were flat ground and well-lit. I followed more slowly, picking my way through the ragged bushes and saplings that gathered near the fence line. Less than halfway up the slope, the wild growth gave way to mowed lawn, and the going was easier, though still as steep.

I had to stop twice to catch my breath before reaching the top. I'd say I need to exercise, but not if it meant getting more fit for illegal activities.

The low hum continued, though the pink afterglow had faded. Oya shook her head. "I can't tell where it's coming from."

I swung my head around, listening carefully. The sound was loudest to our left.

"Ten o'clock," I said.

"Let's go."

As we got further into the cemetery, the hum became more intense. My stomach cramped and I was afraid I was going to pass out or puke or both. I slowed and lost sight of Oya. Now I was alone, and sick, in the dark cemetery.

I tripped on the corner of a stone hidden in the grass and fell forward. I broke my fall with my hands, but my right hand slammed into another stone and pain shot up my arm. I collapsed on the ground, moaning, holding my injured hand. My heartbeat throbbed all the way down my arm to every stunned fingertip.

In moments, my companion had returned. "What kind of a rescue mission is this, where I have to rescue *you*?"

"Not on a mission," I said through clenched teeth. "I'm just..."

"I know, looking for your friend. Well, good news, there are a few people up ahead, and one of them's Fish. He and another guy seem to be tied up right now. Literally."

My heart thumped painfully and I struggled to get my knees under me while I cradled my hand. Blood, warm and sticky, coated my right arm and ran onto my left hand. Fuck it all.

But at least Fish was ahead, and alive. And Castro. He had to be the other person who was tied up.

Why would these people want Castro and Fish? That didn't make sense. And why were they doing something in the cemetery involving a pink flash?

None of it made sense, whatever Oya said or Ware thought. All I needed to do was get up off the ground, get to Castro and Fish, and somehow, with Oya's help, get the two of them out of here. Let the police deal with the others.

Of course, we were all trespassing, so the police would probably want to deal with us as well. But I'd take that over whatever the guy with the ragged ear and his friend wanted to do to Castro.

"Get down," hissed Oya. She pushed on my shoulder and I dropped to my knees behind a grave marker. "Look."

At first, I saw little. The pink glow that had faded so much was still there, but so faint as to be useless.

It took several minutes of waiting for my eyes to adjust even more before I realized the glow had faded because it was being blocked by a door.

I blinked. What was that? Ahead of me was a low hill with what looked like a door cut into the side. I had expected to see more markers.

"What the hell?"

Oya patted me on the shoulder. That sent a spike of pain down my arm and into my injured hand. I hissed

"Sorry," she said. "That's a tumulus. Like a barrow."

That didn't help much, and I didn't really care about technical terms, only about what danger my friends were in.

"Where's Fish and Castro?" I asked. "You said they were tied up."

"They were, or at least Fish was. The other guy was just lying on the ground. The others were standing around outside this tumulus. I guess they've gone inside."

"Inside? Like, inside someone's grave?" My skin crawled at the thought. I didn't like to think about things like graves normally, and this was hardly normal.

"Yes. This is a barrow. Someone wanted to be buried, but not underground, so they piled up the dirt and made a hill and put the person inside. Hence the door into a room beyond."

"Oh." Which was all I could think of to say. *A room beyond?* How messed up was that?

"You seem awfully squeamish." The disapproval in her voice was impossible to miss.

"Maybe you visit graves a lot, but I don't." Hell, I'd never even been to my mother's grave. My aunt had taken care of that and I had avoided having anything to do with the entire deal. It had also been a way of avoiding my aunt and cousin, and I'd managed to avoid them ever since. It's just me and Petunia and Castro.

Who was inside this barrow.

I stood but had to lean against the stone I'd been crouching behind while my head spun from the humming. Oya seemed unaffected.

"How is this not getting to you?" I muttered. "My teeth are about to be jarred out of my head."

She just shook her head. "Just lucky, right?"

Right.

"Maybe you should go first."

For the first time, she hesitated. "I can't," she said with some regret. "Not with this satchel."

The satchel. With whatever-it-was inside.

"You need to go up to the door and see if you can get inside. If it's locked, maybe the key will open it."

"And if not, are you going to do your lock-opening trick again?"

"Maybe. I should be able to get that close."

Should be? Not comforting. But clearly, Castro was only going to get help from me. I closed my eyes a moment and took a deep breath. No matter how much weirder this got, I had to go on. I wasn't going to let Castro down.

I staggered forward drunkenly. The intensity of the wretched humming increased. My eardrums throbbed along with my teeth, and my stomach did slow queasy rolls.

I was glad I hadn't eaten in some hours, or I'd have been puking all over the tombstones around me.

I got up to the door. It had no handle, no knob. I ran my left hand over it, hoping to find a button or keyhole.

Despair trickled into my mind for the first time. Whatever was happening here, it was so far beyond me, how could I even hope to cope with it, let alone fight it for Castro's release? Maybe his very life! After all, Marco Kendall had already died for something that seemed to be inside this burial mound. And what could this damn key go to? So far it had fit nothing.

I pressed against the door and something clicked. I backed up and slowly the door swung open toward me. A pink tendril of light shot out and wrapped around my legs. Other tendrils spread out into the night like tentacles. My immediate thought was of a giant octopus of light trapped underground, reaching out to tug people in toward its voracious maw.

The light tugged me inside, toward a series of steps that led down into the bowels of the cemetery. I tried to resist, but there was no way to stop the pull, no way to stretch the light away from its underground source. Once caught, I had no choice. One way or another, I would find out what was here, at the bottom of the steps. Castro and I would be together, and share whatever fate awaited.

I descended the stairs.

12

The pink tendrils got brighter the farther down I went. I put a hand up to the wall to steady myself against the horrific buzzing that still shook my entire skeleton and every organ, and immediately regretted it. The wall was slick and damp. My fingers came away sticky with the combination of my blood and sweat and the tomb's slime.

The air itself was so wet and hot, I felt as if I were walking through a sauna. I'd been sweating since I'd gotten out of the car, but now rivulets of perspiration ran down my face and neck. At the bottom of the steps, the pink tentacles slid away.

I stood in a room that was brightly lit by the odd pink emanation, which came from the crack between the halves of a sarcophagus. Whatever was glowing, it was inside.

I couldn't even imagine what that could be, nor did I care. I had to find Castro.

It only took a moment to spot him. He was lying on the floor, limp. Was he breathing? I couldn't tell. My heart pounded in my chest as I ran over and dropped to my knees beside him. I touched him and he was warm, and breathing. Relief flooded through me.

I looked around for Fish. He was across the room, sitting awkwardly with his hands behind his back, head bowed. He was looking up at me through long lashes, his expression blank. Had he been hit on the head? Was he concussed?

Two men, the same two men who had been at the bar last night, stared at the sarcophagus, their hands pressed against the top, enraptured by something. The light itself? The thought of what was inside? Who knew?

Who cared? I needed to get Castro out of here. Fish, too, if I could, but Castro was my priority.

I grabbed Castro's hand, wondering if I could pull him to the stairs while the two men were distracted by the noise and the sarcophagus. As soon as I tried to move toward the stairs, though, the light grabbed me again. This time, tentacles wrapped around my chest and waist. They drew me away from Castro.

No! I wouldn't leave him. I struggled but the light only squeezed me more tightly. Defeated for the moment, I went limp. Let the light hold me up while I thought about how to get out of here. The stairwell was several yards behind me and the stairs were steep and wet. It would be difficult, if not impossible, to drag Castro up them alone. I would need Fish's help.

I glanced over at Fish, fearful that he would be too dazed or shocked by whatever injury he had incurred to help. But he was looking directly at me now with a confused expression. I saw him mouth my name as if he couldn't believe I were here.

I jerked my head toward Castro and then toward the stairs. Fish gave me a sorrowful look and a shrug. I wasn't sure what that was supposed to mean.

I was afraid it meant he thought our chances of escape were very slim.

The two men at the sarcophagus lifted their hands away from the lid and stepped back. Immediately, the loud thrumming in the air dropped to background noise.

"That should do it," said the thinner man, the one who had made those delicate, bird-like movements last night in the bar. "All we need now is the mark's blood."

The other man grunted. He turned and saw me. "We have a visitor," he said with a low growl.

The other man turned. "I hardly thought Ware would come himself..." then he noticed it was me. His expression turned quizzical. "The bartender? Ware is sending the best and brightest, I see."

"He didn't send me," I said. "I came for Castro."

"Yes, of course," said the man. He took a step forward. The pink light wrapped around him languidly, then coiled up and away from his shoulders, almost as if he had wings. It was crazy, but I could have sworn I *heard* the flapping of wings now that the tooth-jarring humming had gotten quieter.

"What's going on here?" I demanded. "What have you done with Castro?"

The man flicked his fingers in Castro's direction and Castro moaned. What crazy shit was that?

"I haven't done much...yet," said the man. "I've merely marked him as my own, so that the power that resides in his soul will come to me when he dies. Then I'll have the power to open the gate."

"You're crazy," I said.

The man stepped forward and for the first time I noticed his eyes were lavender, not blue, as I had thought. Or at least they looked that color in the pink light. "I am Marveaux," he said. "And I make perfect sense. You're just an uneducated yokel who will never understand the world as it truly is. And I am not interested in enlightening you. Ware should have done so when he had the chance."

"Can I mark her?" asked the ragged-eared man. "You've already got one."

"No. Two means I have a spare in case something goes wrong."

"You already had two," I said.

"That cretin who found the key?" Marveaux laughed. "He was useless. Most souls are powerless. His wouldn't have done me any good. The only entertainment he could provide was when I watched him gasp out his life on the sidewalk. You can't get enough of that these days. Used to be, you killed a few hundred peasants, no one much cared. Now, the death of even one person can be enough to attract attention."

I was confused. I had meant he had two with Castro and Fish. But Marveaux didn't even seem to notice the other man.

"Where's the key?" asked Marveaux. His lavender eyes narrowed and he felt my pockets. "Where is it?"

"I don't have it," I said. It wasn't much of a lie, but it was all I had.

"Don't know how that damn kid found it," Marveaux growled. "And now for it to keep showing up for *you*."

"She must be lost," said the other man.

"Ridiculous, Garnett," said Marveaux. "Ware wouldn't...oh." A shocked expression crossed his face and he grimaced much as Pellagrio had. The expression was just as alarming on his angular face.

Fish hissed and struggled to stand. "Teryl, no, they can't have it!"

"Ware wouldn't what?" asked the ragged-eared man. Garnett.

Marveaux stepped back and I heard wings flap again. "Ware *would*," he said slowly. "He'd hire someone who was lost and then let her blunder into this without telling her what was happening. That's our Ware."

This time, I heard the capital L on *lost*. I was Lost, whatever that meant.

"Ware's old and tired, and if he thinks his little bartender can help his cause in any way, he is mistaken. She's as mortal and weak as everyone else who works for him."

Fish made a sound that was half-grunt, half-chuckle. "You're wrong. It's almost funny how wrong you are."

As much as I was glad no one was concentrating on me at the moment, it was slightly annoying to be discussed as if I were an inanimate object.

Garnett stepped forward and raised a fist at Fish. "Be quiet, you." This close, the man smelled of onions and garlic and alcohol; I turned my head away from him.

Marveaux leaned in closed and licked my earlobe. "Tasty," he said. "The Lost make the best meals. Now, tell me where you hid the key." He slid one hand down my ribcage while the other snaked around my back. I closed my eyes and shuddered. The tendrils held me too tightly for me to back up, but at the moment, I wasn't sure I could have, anyway. Where Marveaux touched me, my flesh recoiled, but simultaneously, my desire to escape drained away.

It was as if I'd left my body and watched myself be pawed by this man. The unreality of it was dreadful. I opened my mouth to scream but Marveaux covered it with his own. His teeth were sharp. My will slid away.

Why was I struggling? I couldn't remember.

"Stop it!" shouted Fish. "If she had it, she'd tell you."

Marveaux straightened and turned toward my defender, but kept one hand on my side. "You need to be quiet. I'll have what I want, whatever you do. The best you can hope for is that I'm too sated later to pay much attention to you."

Fish shuddered but looked at Marveaux defiantly. "Whatever you have planned, I've suffered worse."

That made *me* shudder. Not just because of what Fish had said, and not even because of how sincerely he'd said it, but because Marveaux accepted the taunt so matter-of-factly. As if he had some idea what Fish had suffered in the past, and knew it was just as horrific as Fish intimated.

Slowly, my thoughts returned to normal. For whatever good it did me, I was myself again. I was Teryl Gray, and I loved Castro, and I was getting us both out of here if I could. And this asshole Marveaux was not going to be able to stop me.

False bravado had to be better than none.

"Garnett will find the key, no matter which one of you it appears near or on," said Marveaux.

"The key will never let you near it," said Fish. "After all this time, it showed up for a mortal teenager, and now it's attached itself to one of the Lost. It's not about to fall into *your* hands."

Marveaux shrugged. "I grew tired of your voice ages ago." He nodded to Garnett, who walked over to Fish and punched him in the face.

Fish was flung backward by the force of the blow. As if that excited the pink light, tentacles darted toward Fish and wrapped around his legs and neck.

Garnett smiled, a genuine "hey, this is fun" smile that made me feel sick. Who were these guys and what in the fucking hell did they really want?

Fish thrashed, but couldn't right himself. He finally lay limp on the floor, breathing hard. A trickle of blood ran down his face toward the stone floor.

"Fuck the key," said Marveaux. He turned away from me and I felt feathers brush against my face.

"We don't need it?" asked Garnett. "I thought we needed it."

"We'll get it eventually," said Marveaux. "Or we'll beat the box open by sheer brute force. Whatever it takes. Now, get the mark."

Garnett nodded and picked up Castro.

"No!" I shouted.

The others ignored me.

Marveaux leaned against the sarcophagus lid and shoved.

Oh, God, he was going to open the damn thing. Visions of moldy bones or, even worse, some kind of horror movie zombie or vampire filled my mind. A tiny voice in the back of my head shouted that zombies and vampires didn't exist, but then, neither did pink light that could wrap itself around you and immobilize you. Neither did keys that magically appeared and disappeared whenever they wanted. Nothing that was happening could, or should, be possible.

Marveaux's entire body was tense with the effort of pushing the sarcophagus lid. What could be in there that he wanted so badly? Gems? Money? A deed for the entire city? I couldn't imagine what could possibly be so important as to make these two men murder people.

Besides which, the presence of mere money wouldn't explain the key, the light, Oya's odd behavior and her squirming satchel, or Ware's offer of "protection."

The sarcophagus lid moved. Just slightly, but the intensity of the light jumped up so suddenly, I had to blink stars out of my vision.

Marveaux and Garnett were so focused on the sarcophagus they didn't notice, as I did, that one of the tentacles holding Fish faded away. As if the stronger the light got, the less able it was to make a coherent, solid form.

None of my bonds had fallen away yet, but now I began testing them again. Their hold was still strong; their cool ropy texture still clung tightly to my arms, my sides, my legs.

The sarcophagus lid moved again. This time, I closed my eyes to shield them from the added brightness.

The humming that penetrated my bones also increased once more. I would have fallen to my knees if the ropes of light hadn't held me up. How long before my bones were literally shaken apart?

I clamped my teeth together to keep from screaming. It was like being in a car riding over a bumpy road times a thousand. Maybe a million.

With a final shove, Marveaux pushed the lid off the top of the sarcophagus. It crashed to the floor in an ear-splitting shriek of rock scraping against and crashing into more rock.

The pink light filled the room. I blinked back the glow as best I could and squinted to see what Marveaux and Garnett would do.

Marveaux reached into the sarcophagus and pulled out a box. A small metal box, almost like the kind of cash box people carried around with them to craft fairs or art shows.

The key went to this box. It had to. This was what Marveaux and Garnett had killed for. Planned to kill for again.

Garnett placed Castro in the sarcophagus. He pulled a knife and held it near Castro's throat. I was in an agony of fear. I had to stop them. I had to get to Castro. I twisted against my bonds with renewed energy.

"Whenever you're ready," Garnett said. The eagerness in his eyes was appalling.

The ropes holding me loosened. Nearby, Fish squirmed out of his own bonds. I moved my arms, then wiggled a foot. I would be bound for only a few more seconds.

Neither of the other men noticed.

Fish launched himself at Garnett, who was surprised into dropping the knife. The large man flung Fish backward, right into Marveaux. Fish and Marveaux went down in a tangle of arms and legs.

I ran toward Garnett who grinned ferociously and launched himself at me. I had no idea what I could do against him, but as his enraged face neared mine, spittle flying, eyes narrowed in the intensity of his joy at doing something brutal, fury exploded in my gut, raced up my spine and took over my mind. I bared my teeth at the man and struck him, open-handed, on the face. Even if he ran over me, even if he broke me, he would know I had landed the first blow.

Pain shot up my arm, as if I'd hit something made of stone. A red-hot stone. I reeled, surprised at the agony. Yes, I'd hit my hand on the tombstone outside, and probably wrenched my shoulder, but *this*...this was far beyond any pain that should be caused by hitting someone.

I lurched to the side and hit the wall, which kept me from collapsing onto the floor. I looked up, expecting to see an enraged Garnett looming in my vision, about to strangle me or rip me to pieces single-handedly.

But he was screaming, hands against his face. As I watched, horrified, his skin turned pale, then faded toward blue and then gray. His body contorted as if he'd suddenly grown extra joints or was being pummeled by an invisible hand.

With a final shriek, he collapsed on the floor and was silent.

I'd done that. How had I done that?

In shock, I looked at Marveaux. Rage suffused his face, but a new emotion was there as well. Fear. He was afraid of me.

Fish, too, looked terrified. I couldn't blame him. The crumpled mess on the floor that had been Garnett twitched once more, then was still.

I had no idea what had just happened. And it scared the fucking shit out of me, too.

13

The tomb was silent. The sudden absence of sound was disorienting. I felt dizzy. I wanted desperately to lie down until the world stopped spinning, but both Fish and Marveaux were staring at me, and Castro was still an unconscious lump trapped in the sarcophagus.

Marveaux finally broke the silence with a chuckle. "Garnett won't soon forgive you for that, but I'm glad to know what I'm dealing with. Ware didn't send you out quite as unarmed as you appear."

"Leave," said Fish. His voice shook. "Don't take anything with you. You know if you harm her, or take that box, Ware will hunt you down."

"Ware's time is past," said Marveaux. He hefted the thing that looked like a cash box under his left arm. "I'm taking this. But first, I'll send a message to Ware."

Fish looked troubled. He managed to pull himself up to his feet again and he stumbled toward Castro. I had no idea what he thought he could do, but I was heartened that, even if something happened to me, Fish would get one of us out of here.

Marveaux pulled out a gun and pointed it at me. "I don't need any tricks to hurt you. You don't have to be uninjured to give me what I want."

God, *who talks like that?* But what can you say to a psychopath with a gun pointed at you?

Fish left Castro and moved in front of me, stumbling and awkward with his hands still tied behind his back. "You'll have to shoot me first."

That made Marveaux laugh. "If you enjoy being gutshot so much, why not?" A blinding flash and a loud bang momentarily blinded and deafened me.

I blinked and slowly, the room came in focus. Fish writhed on the floor in front of me, hands clutching his abdomen. Dark fluid leaked out around his fingers and onto the floor.

Marveaux raised his hands and shouted a word I didn't understand. The light blazed throughout the room and a sudden wind sprang up. It took me a moment to realize it came from the sarcophagus.

But more alarming was that, underneath the sound of the wind, came the sound of sobbing. Except it was coming from me.

"You killed me!" the sobbing voice said, using my mouth. I clapped my hands over my mouth in horror. How could Marco Kendall's voice be coming from me?

I had just crossed the last barrier between sanity and crazy town. There was no other explanation.

Marveaux faltered. "How could you...?"

"Teryl," said Fish through clenched teeth. "You need to use what you have inside you. And use the mark. Between you and Kendall and Ware, you can take this asshole."

A small brass object fell from the ceiling. I automatically held out my hand and caught the key. My key.

A memory flitted past me. *I was exploring alleyways, abandoned parks, junk shops, and fields of debris. Being called by something, unaware of what it was. The sun blazed down on me on an oppressively hot day full of the odors of garbage and car exhaust. And there it was, right there on the surface of a broken slab of asphalt. I had finally found the object that I had dreamed of my whole life. A small key. So unremarkable, and yet so much a part of me. As I picked it up for the first time, I realized it didn't belong to me. I belonged to it.*

How could I remember something like that? Another memory swept over me, of home, and Cara, and a joyful meal of pizza from her favorite restaurant. *Her brown eyes sparkled in the bright light of the kitchen. She picked up the last piece of pizza and laughed at the joke I told her.*

"Teryl! Stop! You'll get lost inside his memories if you keep this up," screamed Fish.

I blinked, disoriented. What was happening?

Marveaux stepped forward and grabbed my hand. His face contorted in rage. "The key. Now."

"Teryl," Fish shouted over the wind, "You have to stop him!"

"Stop him from doing what?" I screamed back as Marveaux wrested the key from my injured hand and stepped back to fit it to the box.

"He needs the contents of the box, and human souls—Castro's soul—and he can create a hellmouth right here."

My mouth dropped open. Crazy town, for sure. But if there were a way to stop someone from opening a mouth to hell, I was all for it.

I threw myself forward and knocked box and key out of Marveaux's hands.

"Bitch!" shouted Marveaux. He scrambled after the key.

"Hey, Teryl, how's it going down there?" Oya's voice floated down from above. She seemed quite calm and sane. How could she not hear what was going on?

"Are you nuts?" I shouted back.

She laughed over noise of the swirling tempest. *Laughed.* "Here," she said. "Take this."

The satchel thumped down the steps. Every time it contacted the floor, something inside screamed.

"What's in there?"

"Don't worry about it," said Oya. "It's nothing important. But touch that bag only with your right hand. *Only your right hand!*"

The bag moved along the floor as whatever was inside it struggled against the straps. The moans that escaped it were clearly human, even though the bag was too small to hold anything but the tiniest infant.

"No!" I shouted. "You do it. I'm getting Castro." I ran to the sarcophagus and grabbed Castro's arms. He wasn't much heavier than me, but he was limp. Dead weight. I was bleeding and had injured my right shoulder and hand. I dropped his arms and worked my arms around his chest while the tempest coming from inside the stone box blew past me. It smelled of dead leaves, and nameless things long forgotten and decayed into dust. I struggled to lift Castro over the lip of the sarcophagus.

"Don't you dare!" said Fish. "You can't save Castro unless you defeat Marveaux. Castro's been marked. Check his hand!"

I looked at Castro's right hand. Sure enough, he sported a black marker squiggle similar to mine, but this one was made up of horizontal lines crossed by chevrons.

"I have to get him out of here."

"Nothing will keep him alive except driving Marveaux away," said Fish.

"Listen to him," shouted Oya. She was at the bottom of the steps now. She pointed to the bag on the floor as Marveaux once again grabbed the small metal box and fitted the key into the lock.

The satchel, which was still inching across the floor, had come very close to me. I could reach it with no effort.

Instinct and nausea warned me away from it. I didn't want to taint my own soul with whatever was in there. Once I picked it up, and committed to using it, my soul would never be clean again. What Oya offered me was damnation.

I didn't even believe in that crap, but I knew it more deeply than I'd ever known anything. I should not touch this bag.

Marveaux screamed in triumph. The box popped open, and he reached inside.

The wind stopped. The sudden absence of the wind made me stumble forward, toward Fish.

Marveaux drew his hand out of the box and held out his prize, a fist-sized pink rock. All this for something that looked like a chunk of quartz? He held the rock in his right hand and pointed it at Castro. Castro moaned as pink light flicked around his skin like sparks. His body twitched and his moaning grew more desperate. Whatever Marveaux and his pink rock were doing, it wasn't good.

The sound of wings came again like a storm, raging around us. It was as if an army of winged creatures were beating the air and yet there was no wind, no wings.

But in the glow of the rock, the shadows of wings were cast onto the wall. Wings that filled the room. Wings that expanded to flick against everything and everyone in the vicinity. The silky soft feeling of feathers brushing against my flesh moved up my arm, across my face. I was frozen in fear.

Castro screamed.

My heart dropped. No matter what, I had to help him. No cost would be too high. I reached out with my right hand, grabbed the satchel, and swung it straight at Marveaux's smirking face.

He screamed as the satchel opened and something launched itself out of the bag, screeching in its own agony. It smelled of damp earth, and the cologne worn by the blond woman in the bar. The one that had walked in just as I was walking out.

A twisted brown form attached to Marveaux's face, shrieking and lashing out in its torment. It barely had a face, but it unmistakably had a wisp of blond hair. It bit at Marveaux, who grabbed it, pulled it off his face with one hand and sank his teeth into its shrunken, paper-like throat.

I held up my hand and called the key to me. It flew through the air and smacked me in the palm. For the briefest moment, I felt the presence of Marco Kendall within me once more, and then his presence shuddered and twisted as if trying to launch itself out of my chest. But it couldn't. It gave a despairing wail, and then it was gone. As if it had never existed.

The scream from the thing on Marveaux's face rose higher and higher until it should have shattered half the glass in the northern portion of the city.

That's a soul, my gut insisted, even as my mind tried to dismiss the entire scene, this entire encounter, as some kind of hallucination. Human souls didn't exist, or, if they did, they didn't look like *that*.

Marveaux dropped the pink stone and the box and wrenched the soul apart with both hands. His facial features stretched and blurred, as if he were changing into something else, something not human.

Something with fangs.

Marveaux threw the pieces of the papery thing away, and they faded into puffs of dirty yellow smoke. But the damage the thing had done was unstoppable. Cracks appeared in Marveaux's flesh, running around his scalp, down his arms. He screamed and stumbled backward as his skin blackened and peeled away.

Fish managed to sit up and point at what Marveaux had dropped.

"Teryl, get the stone back in the box!" shouted Fish. "Do it now!"

I didn't stop to think, I merely obeyed. I grabbed the stone, put it and the key in the box, and slammed the lid shut. Like hell anyone was opening this ever again.

At once, the tomb was plunged into darkness and silence.

14

A lone light came from behind me. I whirled. It was Oya. She'd turned on a flashlight.

She looked at me with approval. "Nice work."

"Fuck that," I said. I ran back to Castro. He mumbled something and reached for my hand. Oya came over and nimbly lifted him out of the sarcophagus and planted him on his feet.

"Are you okay?" I asked.

"What? Where is this?" He sounded sane, at least, and merely confused, not in pain.

"He'll be okay," said Oya.

Fish pushed himself to his feet. "I'll be okay, too. Thanks for asking."

Oya rolled her eyes at him. I stared in disbelief.

"You were shot. You were...you *are* covered in blood. You should be on your way to the hospital." Or, well, he was covered in something. I wasn't willing to give voice to the insane notion it was not blood, but something else entirely.

"I'm harder to kill than most," he said wearily. "Just like Marveaux and Garnett."

I scanned the room but the four of us were the only people I saw. "Where did they go?"

Fish shrugged. "Don't know. Don't care. Just so long as they're not around here again for a while." He looked at Oya. "Ware might be unhappy you lost his prize."

"Nah," said Oya. "He lost one, but he gained at least one more, *and* the box."

"I put the key inside it. You aren't getting it open."

Oya laughed. "Ware doesn't want it *open*."

I couldn't stop shaking. "Stop saying crazy things. I don't know what you're talking about. And what do you mean he lost one but gained one?"

The two of them stared at me. Finally, Fish said, "Look at your hand."

I glanced down at both hands, but what he meant was obvious. The rune that Ware had drawn on my hand had turned into a bright red brand.

"It'll fade," said Fish. "Give it time. It won't ever go away, though. And I don't mean until you die. I mean, *it won't ever go away*. When you bled onto it and then used it, you fused it to your flesh, and that can't be undone. When it was merely drawn on, you could have gotten it off. Once you hit Garnett with a blood-mark, you sealed your fate."

I wrapped my left arm around Castro's shoulders. It was far past time to get him out of here and away from these nutcases. "Whatever. I'm going to take him home now, and the two of you...do whatever it is you want. I'm leaving."

"See you tomorrow night," said Fish.

"No," I said. "How can I go back there after tonight? You are all insane."

"You won't be able to go anywhere else, not now," said Oya sadly. "With Ware's mark seared into your flesh, you won't be allowed to remain on the sidelines. You're on a side now."

"I'm not on anyone's side."

"Whether you want to be or not, you are," said Fish.

"Fuck you. Fuck you both."

"That sounds like fun," said Oya as I passed her. "I'll keep it in mind."

Castro leaned on me and mumbled something, but I didn't understand him. I just wanted to get him out of here.

At the top of the stairs, I realized I now had to get Castro down the steep, grass-covered hill and through the gate. Me, the born stumblebum. I shook him slightly. "Hey, look, you can lean on me, but I can't take your weight all the way down the hill. Give me some help here."

He did his best, but we half-slid, half-walked down the slope. It took me a few minutes to find the open gate and get Castro through it, and we crossed Hall Street. My car was only yards away.

I got Castro into the car, shut the door and turned around.

And gasped. Ware stood there, as broad as usual, but even more forbidding. I knew he hadn't been there moments before.

"What? How?"

He put a hand on my shoulder. His face reflected sadness, and perhaps a little anger. Inside, I shrank from that anger, even though some inner instinct told me it wasn't directed at me.

"I'm sorry, Teryl," he said. He glanced at the cemetery. "Little Girl will bring me the box, so that won't trouble you anymore. It's time we talked. Tomorrow, come to your shift a few minutes early. We'll go into my office and discuss your new situation. It ought to come with a raise, don't you think?"

It took a few seconds to get my tongue in gear, and a moment more to realize he'd said *go into my office*. The place that had been forbidden to me previously. I shuddered, but managed to say, "A raise is the least of it."

He nodded. "I understand. Go home now, get some rest." He glanced in the car at Castro. "He'll be fine, and probably won't remember a thing."

"Convenient."

He shrugged and dropped his hand. "We couldn't operate very well in the open if people remembered all their dealings with us."

Us? I didn't even want to know what that meant. Maybe later, but not now. My entire soul longed for home and a night lying next to Castro, who was alive and all right.

I also needed to be grunted at in greeting by Petunia. I needed that more than I could say.

"And me? Will I forget?"

He looked over my shoulder and grimaced, as if he couldn't say this to my face. "No. You're special, Teryl. I always knew it. It's why I hired you. I wanted you on my side willingly. Now you're mine, whether you want to be or not."

"You're not making any more sense than Fish and Oya."

His eyebrows shot up. "She gave you a name to call her? That's a surprise."

"Don't care," I said. "I'm leaving."

He nodded and stepped back. I got into the car and drove through the open gate, turned left onto Hall Street.

I glanced back only once, in time to see Oya give Ware the box while Fish watched, hands still pressed against his abdomen. Then the three of them turned as one and watched me drive away. Oya towered over both the men, but even so, it was clear who had the true power in that trio.

My right palm had tingled the moment Ware touched the box. I didn't know how or why, exactly, but Ware and I were connected, and that thought turned my stomach.

Ware was part of me now, and I hated the thought. But even more, I hated myself. I had destroyed two people. Two souls. I'd done something to Marco Kendall. It was as if I'd *eaten* him. Used him up until he was nothing but a husk, and the husk had dissolved away. I had the sinking feeling that I could have done more with him, if I'd only known how. *Used him.*

That thought frightened me to the tips of my toes.

And the woman. She was gone, too. I didn't know her name, but I knew she had been erased from the universe. And the only people I knew who could have told me more about her, like Ware and Oya, did not care what had happened to her. She had been nothing to them. How could I work for, or even hang around with, people like that?

If *people* were even the right word.

Castro mumbled something again. I put my hand on his. For tonight, the craziness was over, and home was only a few miles away.

I drove on through the night, under the streetlights of the city, and tried not to hear the sound of wings overhead.

About the Author

 Marella Sands is a native St. Louisan who has published two historical novels, several short stories, and non-fiction works. Her historical novels, *Sky Knife* and *Serpent and Storm*, were set in 5th century Central America. *Sky Knife* has also appeared in a German edition as *Der Mayapriester*. In addition, she co-wrote two King's Quest novels with fellow St. Louisan Mark Sumner under the name Kenyon Morr. She has had short stories in several recent anthologies. She has always been interested in cemeteries, and sits on the board of one. She and her husband travel whenever they can and stop by old cemeteries when they have the opportunity.

Marella earned degrees in anthropology from the University of Tulsa and Kent State University. The author's household includes the author, her husband, and a multitude of pets.

Word Posse Fun Fact

For years, I've wanted to write a story with a bartender as the main character, but I couldn't decide what the story would be about or even if the bartender would be male or female. All I knew was that weird stuff would happen and the owner of the bar would be a mysterious figure cloaked in supernatural power. While I was mulling that over, I took a bartending class (though I've never actually had a job tending bar) and have visited places like the Highland Park distillery in the Orkneys. I've sampled a few dozen whiskeys, but there are still so many to try. So much to taste, so little time.